THE BEAST WITHIN

Mended Souls #2

USA Today Bestselling Author
Jacquie Biggar

ISBN: 978-1-988126-09-8

Dedication

I want to dedicate this book to the thousands of aboriginal women who have gone missing in Canada.

May you find peace in the warmth of Heaven's embrace.

Jacquie Biggar

I can calculate the motion of heavenly bodies, but not the madness of people.

Isaac Newton

What Readers are Saying

The Guardian

Who wouldn't want to be swept off her feet by a movie star? And championed by a guardian angel? Sign me up! And like any great start to a series, the ending left me reaching for the next book. Highly recommended
Christine Hart

I was lucky to receive an advanced copy of The Guardian. A quick, easy read that I enjoyed!. A serious topic handled not only with touching moments but a few humorous moments also. Romance, suspense, family ties, friendship, angels that aren't sure about being angels, some sad moments, some nail biter moments, and a darling dog named Sugar Bear....what more could we want? I'm looking forward to the next book in this series.

Barbara Cassata

* * *

The Sheriff Meets His Match

Who could possibly be the perfect match for Sheriff Jack Garrett, the steadfast pillar of a small west coast town like Tidal Falls? Enter Laurel Thomas, a woman on the run from her past in Florida. As soon as she shows up in Tidal Falls, she turns Jack's meticulously organized world upside down with her disorganized ways, sexy looks and feisty humor. I'd been craving Jack's story every since I read about him in an earlier story in the Wounded Hearts series, and I wasn't disappointed! Ms Biggar's characters leap off the page and become family you'll be rooting for with all your heart.

Jacqui Nelson

I really enjoyed this romance. It has a heroine that's running around helping family, while working for the sheriff. She uses sticky notes to help keep everything straight, while the family tends to count on her to make everything right. This is full of humor and a little bit of serious in a small town type setting. I've given it a rating of 4.5*. It really made me laugh.

Nancy Luebke

* * *

Twilight's Encore

What a captivating story. Twilight's Encore is the third book

of Wounded Hearts series. This is Ty's and Katy's story, i have

to say what a beautiful story!!!

Nicole- Reading Alley

This is a very heartwarming, suspenseful book that will have you cheering for the good guys. HIGHLY RECOMMEND and Can't wait for Book 4 in the Wounded Hearts series.

Barbara

* * *

The Rebel's Redemption

What I loved about this story was not only the premise but how it all came together.

LAS reviewer

THE REBEL'S REDEMPTION (Wounded Hearts, #2) by Jacquie Biggar had me reading this romantic suspense well past my bedtime. The characters are so well written they could walk right off the page!

Avonna-The Romance Reviews

Other Books by This Author

Wounded Hearts Series

Tidal Falls

The Rebel's Redemption

Twilight's Encore

The Sheriff Meets His Match

Summer Lovin'

Wounded Hearts Box Set

Mended Souls Series

The Guardian

The Beast Within

Standalones

Silver Bells- Coming Soon

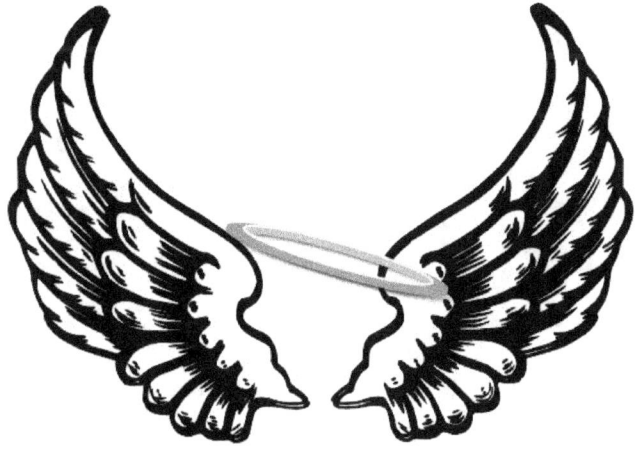

Preface

She didn't expect to land in the crosshairs of a serial killer.

Can two displaced angels save a woman from the clutches of a vicious killer?

Julie Crenshaw is offered work on Vancouver Island and grabs on like a lifeline.

She didn't expect to land in the crosshairs of a serial killer.

Connor O'Rourke has seen his share of human depravities during his fourteen years as a homicide detective, but is still sickened by the murderer terrorizing his island shores.

And threatening his key witness.

As the stakes rise, can two people give love a second chance?

Or will a killer be the winner?

PROLOGUE

Her skin was tender as the belly of a kitten. And just as fragile.

Her screams edged toward hysteria, muffled by the material of her slutty shirt. He'd taken pleasure in cutting the offensive cloth from her body and stuffing it into her cherry red mouth.

Almond shaped eyes, the color of strong black coffee and wide with terror, glittered with the tears streaming down her dusky cheeks.

Too late for that. She should have begged for mercy when he demanded it. Instead, she'd laughed at him.

She wasn't laughing now.

He ran a finger from the gold love knot piercing her belly button, up to coffee-colored breasts tipped with cocoa nipples peaked with fear. She should be scared. He was her master and she'd wronged him. She had to pay.

He grinned.

This was his favorite part. There was probably something wrong with him, but the thrill he got out of having complete control over his subjects filled his body with adrenaline, made blood rush to his extremities, and turned him rock hard. Way better than sex. Sex was dirty, all that sweat and bodily fluids. Not this. This was clean—spiritual.

He picked up the red hot iron he'd been heating on the propane stove. When she saw what he had in his hand, her body bowed against its bonds, but there was no escape. She'd run away from him for the last time.

He pinched her pebbled nipple, tipping her breast upward so he could access the tender skin beneath. The acrid scent of burning flesh and the inhaled silent scream of torture before her eyes rolled back in her head rewarded him for his patience. The *S* was perfectly shaped. The snake's head crested the top of the curve, its forked tongue curling around the scorched meat of her breast.

She was his now.

Chapter one

Except for the gentle lapping of waves against the shoreline, the beach was quiet. Eerily quiet. Julie Crenshaw picked up a flat stone and threw it into the chilly Pacific Ocean. It plunged through the gently rolling waves like a swimmer fighting the tides. She watched for a moment, then continued down shore.

The sun was little more than a thought on the horizon, shading the sky with the faintest hint of what was to come. Oranges, yellows, and a blush of pink like a young girl's cheeks. The sand was still damp from the recent high tide and washed clean of tracks.

She loved this time of morning. The briny scent of the ocean cleared her head and prepared her for the day to come. A few Canadian Geese flew overhead, their distinctive honk blending with the sound of the surf, just as a gull rose a few feet away, a crab squirming in its beak and the red and white lighthouse stood sentinel, warning sailors of the dangerous rocks hidden just beneath the surface.

Julie counted her blessings because she was able to live in such beautiful surroundings, but it was bittersweet. The plan had been for her and Mike to move here together, but a drunk driver had ended those dreams forever.

Time to leave; she had a long day in front of her. The beach was littered with driftwood from the recent winter storms. Thick logs and tree stumps made for slow going back to the car. She was nearing the grassy verge when her gaze caught on something in a hollow under a four-foot stump. She couldn't see any eyes staring back at her so it probably wasn't a predator. Relieved, she nonetheless kept a good grip on the stick she'd been using to walk through the sand. "Quit being a chicken, let's just check it out then."

She crouched and gazed timidly into the hollow. It looked like the sole of a shoe. Curious, she tugged, and with a bit of effort a sneaker came loose. When she saw what was inside the shoe, Julie screamed.

CHAPTER TWO

Julie glanced over her shoulder at the crowd of interested onlookers behind the police barricades, and shivered. Any enjoyment she'd taken in the start of her day was long gone. It was one thing to report about crime as part of her daily job; it was another thing entirely to be a witness to a possible homicide.

Cuddling a little deeper into the jacket one of the patrolmen had thrown about her shoulders, she watched the beehive of activity around the tree stump and fervently wished herself a hundred miles away. She should probably be trying to get some statements from the investigating officers, but she couldn't seem to shake the shock. It wasn't the first dead body she'd ever seen. In her job she often trailed those first on scene and ended up with an eyeful. But this… this was out of her comfort zone. Way out.

"You the witness who found the severed foot?" A brusque masculine voice asked from behind.

Startled, she turned and looked into steely gray eyes set in a face that was more interesting than handsome. Crow's feet suggested he spent a lot of time squinting into the sun, as did the ochre cast of his skin. His jaw was square and unyielding and drew the eye to lips set in a hard, straight line.

"Yeah, lucky me," she muttered.

Those lips tilted, hinting at humor, then firmed up again. Julie lifted her gaze and met his sympathetic stare. She stiffened. She'd seen that look way too many times after Mike died. She hated it.

"When can I go home? I have to get to work."

The man's eyes narrowed. "I'm sure your boss will understand. Unless you have something to hide?"

The guy didn't like to waste words.

"I didn't catch your name?"

"O'Rourke. Detective Connor O'Rourke."

Guess that explained his interest in her.

Quelling her odd disappointment, Julie got straight to the facts. "Well, *Detective*, there's not a lot I can tell you. I was out for my morning walk and caught sight of… something that didn't belong."

She shuddered, remembering again her horror at the first glimpse of what was in that running shoe. "Anyway, as soon as I realized what it was, I called 911, and you guys showed up. End of story. Can I go now?"

O'Rourke pulled a notebook and pen out of an inside jacket pocket, affording her a glimpse of a muscular chest covered in a tight fitting navy blue t-shirt, and shoulder holster. She gulped.

"I'm going to need a name and address," he said.

"Whatever for?" she protested. "I've told you everything I know."

"Let's just say I like to cover my bases," he replied, and clicked the pen open.

Julie sighed. There was no way to avoid this— unless she faked her name? Tempting as it was, she knew it would only make matters worse.

"Julie Crenshaw, 2011 Keating Cross Road." She didn't have long to wait—aaaaaand there it was, the light bulb moment. He looked up, startled, renewed interest and curiosity igniting those mercury eyes.

"As in, Lucas Carmichael, the movie star? You're the woman who survived the accident?"

Why did everyone always look so amazed by that? She should be used to that reaction by now, but it still had the power to sting.

"Yes, detective, Mike Crenshaw was my husband. Is that all?" She didn't really care if she was being rude any more. She tugged off the officer's coat and handed it across to O'Rourke. "If you need any more information you can reach me at the VIBS news station, I'm one of their investigative journalists."

She turned to leave, and frowned at the news vans lined up on the road beyond the straining crowd. Great, her boss was going to have her head on a platter.

Sighing, she tugged her cell phone from her pocket and clicked on the recorder function before swinging back to the detective—and caught him checking out her butt.

Her cheeks heated. She raised her brow. He shrugged, and glowered at the phone.

"Put that away, Mrs. Crenshaw. There will be no statements for the press at this time."

"So the rumors are true then?" she asked. "This isn't the first discovery of this nature, Detective. Don't you owe the public an explanation?"

He snapped the notebook closed and shoved it in his pocket, the black leather of his coat pulling taut over his biceps. The clouds that had been gathering all morning started to spit rain, turning his auburn hair a rich chocolate brown.

He glanced at the crime scene, and then up to the sky, no doubt worried about losing his evidence to Mother Nature.

"Look, I gotta get back there. Just keep this under your hat until we find out what we're dealing with, okay?" He nodded to the crowd. "Need help getting through that?"

Oddly touched that he would think of her comfort, she shook her head. "I'm good."

O'Rourke nodded, then strode away, his long jean-clad legs eating up the distance to the group examining every square inch of the area around the stump. Talk about your needle in a haystack. Between the ebb and flow of the tides, the wildlife and the sand, they were fighting impossible odds.

She climbed the slight incline to the string of yellow ribbon and waited for an officer to clear the way. Regardless of her words, these people knew something bad had happened and they wanted information.

A senior with earphones dangling from her sweat-suit called, "What happened?"

Another person, his hand wrapped around the handle of a cane asked, "Why are the police down there? Did someone kick the bucket?"

Well, that's one way of putting it.

She knew better than to say anything. They'd never let her go if she did, so she just kept her eye on the prize—her little Honda Civic sitting far to the left of the line of vehicles. Some of the competitor news teams tried to get a statement out of her, but she only smiled and kept moving. And then she saw them. Her cameraman, Rudy, and their driver, Sam. They were set up on the shore, filming up the beach to the location of the find.

Julie hurried over, relieved to see her friends.

"I was wondering if you heard," she said when she was near enough for them to hear over the mix of vehicles passing on the roadway, and the surf.

Rudy grinned. "Are you kidding? Taylor had us out here almost before it happened."

Sam swept her into a hug. "You had us worried. We could see that cop interrogating you. Oh, honey, are you okay?"

Julie closed her eyes and pictured O'Rourke's uncompromising face. "I'm fine. How did you guys hear?"

Sam leaned back, her usually laughing blue eyes, serious. "Taylor told us you made the call. You know her, she has connections everywhere."

True. It often gave them an advantage over the other news stations, something they all appreciated.

"So, was it bad?" Rudy asked. Typical male, looking for the gory details.

"Let her be," Sam scolded her husband. "She'll tell us when she's ready." Then she totally ruined it by looking at Julie with huge puppy-dog eyes.

She laughed. "You two deserve each other, one's as bad as the other." Then, before they could protest, she added, "It was the shock more than anything. It was mostly bone, and still lodged in the shoe so I didn't see much." A random shiver squirmed down her spine.

"Well, I think you're incredibly brave. If it were me, I probably would have fainted right there." Sam said.

Julie shrugged, uncomfortable. She wasn't feeling very brave.

"You guys about done? I want to get to the station and do a little research."

Rudy set his camera in its bag and started dismantling his tripod. "We'll be right behind you. I think I have enough here."

Julie nodded and headed for her car. She opened her door. Just before she climbed in, she took one last look down the beach. But there was no sign of Mr. Tall, Dark, and Annoyingly Handsome.

CHAPTER THREE

O'Rourke rubbed the back of his neck and glared at the looming rain clouds. The last thing he needed was a storm messing with his crime scene. His team scoured the sand dunes, leaving virtually no grain unturned. He'd handpicked them for this case. They were all veteran officers and knew their shit. Good thing because this was the third severed foot found in as many months. He hated to even think the S word, but it looked increasingly inevitable.

Serial Killer.

Two words guaranteed to strike fear into anyone's heart.

Their perp was smart. He'd made good use of the ocean tides with the briny water, sand, and predators doing their share to destroy the remains. They'd left little in the way of evidence behind other than a severed foot in a shoe.

Questions were mounting and the press were after him for answers he didn't have. He turned and passed a tired glance over the news vans, wishing he could will them away. The woman had neared the end of the line and was getting ready to climb into a beat up old white Civic. His pulse jumped. She called to a guy dismantling a camera tripod, then opened the door to get in, but hesitated long enough for a last look down the beach.

He took an instinctive step forward, his hand lifting to catch her attention. Something elemental arced between them like a static charge. Then she climbed into her car and drove away without a backward glance and he lowered his hand, clenching it by his side.

Well, what did he expect? Just because he'd been hit by the attraction bug didn't mean the feeling was mutual. And even if it had been, now was not the time.

"Boss." A white-suited tech held up a baggie.

Connor grimaced and picked his way over the rocks and driftwood washed up from the surf. He had a good idea what they were going to find before he even got there. This guy liked to play games.

"Is it the same?" He held out his hand, not surprised to see a puzzle piece in the bottom of the bag.

"Yeah," the tech said. "Edge piece, the name *Cindy* written lefthanded in cursive with black permanent marker on the back."

Approximately one-inch long, another side piece, this one dark gray with shadowy lines running the length. The other two pieces had come from different parts of the puzzle, though the coloring suggested it was the same picture. The first one had the name Amanda, the second Betty. He was toying with them, leaving clues to the victims names, Con was sure of it. He just couldn't prove anything. Yet.

They were running names through the NCMPUR Operations—The National Centre for Missing Persons and Unidentified Remains. But with two of the three victims First Nations women their job was twice as hard. With over one thousand missing Aboriginal women alone, and pressure from their communities as well as the Federal government to get a handle on these crimes, Connor was under a lot of stress. Add to that the island was just coming into tourist season, and this whole thing just became a nightmare.

"Get this back to the lab. See if we can get lucky for a change. Even a partial would give us something to go on." More than they had now.

"Okay, boss." The tech took the baggie, labeled it, and stuck it in a black duffel before hurrying away.

Connor gazed out at the storm-tossed waves, his stomach twisting in knots, then sighed and made his way over to the group studying the grisly remains. The Medical Examiner, a silver-haired man in his late fifties, glanced up from his examination, and gave a short nod.

"Detective."

"What do you have for me, doc?" Con dropped to his haunches and choked back bile at the gruesome sight of a sinewy ankle bone, tendons still attached, poking out of a dirty white and blue canvas running shoe.

"Size seven, women's. Hard to tell until we get the test results back, but I'd have to say Aboriginal from the flat arch and the shape of the phalanges." His gaze was grave. "It's the left foot again, Connor."

Shit.

The team had taken extra care to keep that information under wraps. The last thing they needed was a copy-cat.

Until now they'd assumed the missing feet were a coincidence, maybe caused by suicides. Jumpers as they called them—people who chose to end their lives by jumping off bridges—sometimes washed up on the coast, their bodies decayed by their time in the water. But with it being the same foot and those damn taunting puzzle pieces, it was becoming obvious this was the work of a killer.

He nodded and rose. "Thanks, doc." A quick glance at his watch revealed they'd already been here a couple of hours. Most of the news teams had given up, leaving a skeleton crew behind to pick his bones, if he let them. He had no intention of doing so.

"I'm heading back to the office. You guys good?"

"Yep."

"Sure thing."

"When's lunch?" This from Esposito, the walking garbage can. The guy was always hungry, didn't matter how much he ate, and skinny as a rail.

Connor grinned. "Prudence didn't fill your bottomless gut this morning?" They'd only been married six months and were still in the honeymoon phase, as he liked to call it.

"Nah, she wasn't feelin' too good," Dan said, his brow furrowed. "Hey, you don't suppose...?"

Con stifled his envy and clapped his friend on the back. "What are you asking me for? Go home and see your wife, Dan. Give her a hug from me. The rest of the team can finish up here."

Dan looked at the shoe, the excitement dimming from his gaze. "We gotta catch this bastard, Con."

His buddy climb the embankment to his patrol car, leaving Connor haunted by the thought of three women who would never get the opportunity to share another moment with their loved ones.

***

Newly minted angel Lucas Carmichael sat in the back seat of his quarry's rattletrap car and grimaced. He needed a lead on her dead husband, but didn't know how he was going to get it.

The woman's attention was on the action down the beach. Men dressed in paperwhite suits with little white booties on their feet roamed up and down the beach like a horde of flies. He didn't know what they were doing, and he didn't care—all he wanted was Natalya. And the only way to find her was the woman getting into the front seat of the car.

Julie Crenshaw.

She looked a lot better than the last time he'd seen her. On that occasion fright had twisted her face into a Halloween mask of horror as their vehicles hurtled toward an unavoidable collision.

Eighteen months had given her skin a peachy, healthy glow. She leaned forward to start the ignition and her hair flowed over her shoulder in bright golden-brown waves. All except for one thin streak of silver, like a moonbeam stuck in the strands behind her ear.

She shifted into gear and glanced over her shoulder to back onto the road. Lucas froze, though of course she couldn't see him in his angel form.

"We need to hurry. The boys will be home from school soon."

Lucas sucked in a harsh breath. Was she talking to him?

"C'mon car, don't let me down now."

Her car. She was talking to her car. He smiled, liking this woman who had been through so much in the last year-and-a-half. If not for his split second of inattention while driving, none of the preceding month's events needed to have happened.

But that in no way excused the boy's father for stealing away with the love of Lucas' life.

Someone had to pay.

CHAPTER FOUR

"You may as well sit down, you're not going anywhere."

The masculine voice rumbled from the darkest reaches of the cave. The beast had returned.

Natalya wrapped suddenly cold arms around her body and slowly turned to meet her enemy's gaze. He stood near the back of the stone cavern, in a section she'd searched inch by tortuous inch. She would have sworn there was nothing there other than the well where she drew water and the rustic bathroom he must have built in preparation for her stay. How did he get in?

"You can't keep me here forever," she snapped, though he was doing a damn fine job of it so far. With no windows the only source of light in this godforsaken pit was the candles she'd found on a shelf against one side of the eight-by-ten room. She knew the exact dimensions; had spent more than enough time pacing the makeshift prison. After two months of scratching out calendar marks whenever she estimated another day had passed, she'd given up.

But not her dreams of escape.

"I brought food. Sit." The hulking brute dropped a bag onto the rough wooden table and pulled out a chair, lowering himself down with a heavy sigh. "C'mon, I won't bite."

So he says.

Nat edged closer, her stomach knocking against her backbone, but unwilling to place herself in any more danger. Normally he brought the food while she slept, so she rarely saw him—hours, days, alone with nothing more than visions of the past to haunt her dreams.

Lucas.

He would be half out of his mind with worry. Ever since she could remember he'd been their guardian, hers and Scott's. Small wonder she'd carried a severe case of hero worship for the gangly boy who'd befriended the new kids on the block and stepped in to protect them from the neighborhood bullies. As they grew the adoration changed to attraction, and attraction to love. Not that he'd known, or would have appreciated it if he had. He and Scott had bonded like brothers and both men made it their priority to shelter her from everything, whether abusive parents or amorous boyfriends.

The flame on the white candle flickered and danced, the wax leaving fat globs like tears drying on the side, and shadows jumping on the wall. Her abductor barely acknowledged her presence, his attention on the heaping plate of crispy chicken pieces in front of him. He took a big bite out of a leg, his white teeth flashing in the light. He wiped his lips with the back of his hand, then pushed the plate her way.

"Eat. I don't need you getting sick again."

Natalya stiffened. The *illness* he spoke of was his fault. If he hadn't attacked Lucas and then shoved her when she tried to stop it, she wouldn't have fallen and smashed her head against the hearth. When she'd woken up days later, she'd been here, in purgatory.

Defiant, she snatched the biggest piece of chicken she could find and took a mouthful, her gaze defying him to comment. He only grunted and continued to chew on his own food. For a while silence reigned while basic necessities took over. She'd forgotten how a simple thing like tasty chicken could make her feel. Alive. Human.

Something she'd never be again.

Appetite gone, Nat threw her scraps into the bag and wiped her fingers with one of the napkins on the table. Goosebumps crawled up her spine and broke across her arms as her fingers stuck to the paper. Hmm, so much for losing phobias after you died.

She eyed the man finishing his meal and wondered what his biggest fear was, and how could she use it to get out of this mess.

"He'll find me, you know," she said. "Lucas won't give up. Why don't you take me back and we can forget this ever happened?"

Yeah, like she could forgive or forget the months of solitary confinement this brute had subjected her to. It wasn't her fault he'd lost his family. It wasn't anyone's fault. The accident had destroyed lots of lives.

"I don't want him to give up," he growled. "I want him to suffer."

He pushed away from the table, the chair catching on the thick pile of the carpet lining the floor. The candle hissed and sputtered as he rose to his full height, casting a dark shadow across the wall.

Natalya's heart jumped and she backed up a couple of steps before she could stop herself. She clenched sweaty hands into fists and glared. "Why are you doing this? It won't bring your family back."

His head reared as though from a blow. He stared at the ceiling, his jaw clenched and throat working. His gaze when he turned it on her a few moments later burned with green fire. "You think I don't know that?"

He kicked the chair and it went over with a crash. "I live with that fact every god-damn day. I will never hold my children again. Or teach them to drive. Or be best man at their weddings." He pinched the bridge of his nose and sucked in a harsh breath. "And then there is my wife."

The raw pain in his eyes was agonizing to see.

"Jules dreamed of having a little girl. She loved the boys so much, but a girl…" He turned away, his shoulders hunched under the weight of his loss. "We were choosing a name for the baby that day."

His words were so low Nat had to lean closer to hear him. She lifted a hand to offer comfort, then slowly let it drop. He wouldn't appreciate it coming from her—the enemy.

"I'm sorry," she whispered, at a loss as to what she could say that might ease his agony.

His back stiffened and he turned on her, his hands fisted. "I don't want your apologies," he snarled. "All the *sorrys* in the world won't bring my family back to me."

He strode to the rear wall of the cave, then hesitated, his gaze almost regretful as it rested on her.

"The food will last you for a few days. I'll be back with more."

Natalya couldn't help it, the thought of being all alone sending her stumbling forward. "Please," she begged. "Let me go."

He shook his head and lifted a hand, freezing her in her tracks. A dark hole opened in the wall and he stepped through, the opening sliding closed behind him.

The force field eased and Nat fell to her knees, tears sliding down her cheeks. She crawled over and desperately clawed at the rock face but couldn't find any triggers to let her out. She kept trying long after her fingers were cut and bleeding and jagged sobs turned her throat as raw and aching as her hands.

CHAPTER FIVE

Julie pulled into the paved driveway and parked in front of the single car garage just as the school bus stopped down the street and let off a rag-tag bunch of laughing, talking kids. All except her boys, last to step down from the vehicle. They barely glanced up from their inspection of the sidewalk when the doors slid closed and the bus signaled away from the curb.

She sighed and waited while they trudged the half block to their front gate. There were no waves or yelled plans to join the other kids in a game of street hockey after their dinner. No suggestions of an impromptu basketball match using the hoop above the garage door, or a bike ride to the nearby park. Nothing at all. In fact, Dustin looked like he had another of his perpetual mad-ons happening, with hunched shoulders and downcast expression.

Meanwhile, Freddie tagged along behind, casting envious glances at the neighbor boy running down the street toward the others setting up for the hockey game.

"Why can't we, Dusty?" Freddie tugged on his older brother's jacket, barely slowing him down. "I want to play."

Dustin stopped short, glaring at the laughing kids down the block. "They're a big bunch of dummies." He kicked at a stray pebble, sending it skittering down the walk.

Julie hiked her satchel higher on her shoulder and closed the car door. Dustin glanced her way, then trudged into the house without a word.

Julie's welcoming smile flat-lined, her son's continuing anger creating a hard ball of tension in her gut. She'd taken him to counselling after his father's death, but it hadn't done much to alleviate the guilt he carried. He felt the accident was his fault and nothing Julie could say would change his mind.

"Mom, can I go play?" Freddie giggled as the neighbor's dog dropped a beat up ball glove at his feet.

She forced a cheerful expression and held out her arms. "Do I get a cuddle first?"

Young enough not to care who might be watching, he ran into her embrace, his chubby arms wrapping her waist in a bear hug. She held on a moment too long, reluctant to give up the scent of bubblegum and sun that clung to his soft skin.

"Mom, you're squeezing me to death," he laughed into her chest.

She gave one last clench, half teasing, half desperation, and let him go. "Be back in an hour, and watch out for traffic."

"Okay, love you, Mom," he said, grabbing the glove and heading for the street, his attention already half a block away.

"Love you, son," she answered, and he was gone. Leaving her alone. Deflated.

She turned for the house, coming to a halt when she noticed Dustin standing on the other side of the screen. There was that knot again. Much as she loved her eldest son, Julie hated the undercurrents that ran between them like a tide of noxious gas. He'd been daddy's boy, had followed Mike wherever he went, questions flying a-mile-a-minute. They'd often joked that the only time Dusty was quiet was when he was asleep.

Mike.

She missed her husband every day. The guilt bit again.

In the beginning, after the accident, the combined loss of their unborn daughter and husband and father had left the three of them lost. Floundering in a mire of heartbreak, depression, and agony. Her boss and best friend, Taylor Monroe, had recommended family counselling. But it was only when Dustin ran away and was almost killed by the agent of the man who crashed into them, movie star, Lucas Carmichael, that she agreed. It turned out to be the right decision. It hadn't happened overnight, but slowly she and the boys came back from the deep pit of loss they'd fallen into. And when Taylor was offered a temporary promotion too good to pass up—in Canada—she'd persuaded Julie to make a fresh start and move with her.

Julie balked. Her husband was buried in Graceland Cemetery, their daughter in the same plot. How could she leave them? But then she'd looked into Dustin's green eyes and his stubborn attitude, Freddie's cowlick and love of life, and she realized Mike would always be with them, wherever they were.

"Don't you want to go with your brother, Dusty?" she cajoled, hoping to tempt him out of his funk.

He stared at her, his eyes almost an eerie green through the dark screening. "I have homework."

Well, that was a first. Usually she had to fight with them to do their schoolwork. She climbed the cement steps, vaguely noticing her planters filled with hydrangeas needed watering. Dustin turned away and slunk into the living room. He flopped onto the couch, picked up the remote, and turned on the television, ignoring her when she entered the house.

Julie was just about to remonstrate him when the news came on and there she was, front and center.

Dustin glanced at her curiously, then refocused on the report, turning up the volume to subsonic.

A competing news team had the story out on the early news broadcast. Taylor was going to be pissed.

She watched in dismay as they panned over the beach and the swarms of police and technicians, before sweeping out to encompass the crowd. They obviously didn't know she'd found the remains—that was something at least. But the cameraman had zeroed in on her as she stood talking to the detective, so it was only a matter of time.

O'Rourke carved as imposing a figure on TV as he did in real life. His eyes matched the stormy skies behind his head. With a forbidding jawline and those scowling lips it's a wonder she'd been able to link two words together. The camera stayed on him when she hurried off and Julie shivered under the intensity of his gaze.

Uncomfortable, she reached over and snagged the remote, turning off the TV.

"What was that about?"

Great. The first genuine sign of interest Dustin had shown her in months and she couldn't share the news.

She leaned over and rumpled his hair, as tow-headed as his father's. "Oh, you know, work. What should we have for dinner?"

He stared at her for a long moment, hurt flashing like bursts of lightning in his eyes, then he grabbed his workbook and opened it up, effectively blocking her out. "I'm not hungry. I gotta get this done, so…"

Nice. Shot down by an eight-year-old.

***

Connor spent the rest of the morning poring over cold case files, hoping something would jump out at him and give them a place to start. Many of the missing women left their homes in hope of a better existence and instead found themselves living on the streets. Some had drifted into alcohol and drug abuse, while others were taken in by men who offered them the good life in return for a few favors.

The 'Johns' had mob connections and could ship the girls from one end of the country to the other, some even ending up Stateside or farther. Added to these complications was the delicate matter of dealing with international law. The FBI preferred to handle things their way and only shared information on a case by case basis. Understandable, but not helpful in this instance.

They were all after the same thing. To catch a murderer.

"How's the case coming?"

Connor glanced away from the computer and blinked the room back into focus. His partner, Matthew Roy, slouched on the corner of his desk, a donut in one hand, Styrofoam cup of coffee in the other.

He waved the donut at the screen before taking a bite. "I heard it was a bad one."

Connor grimaced and wiped the trail of crumbs into the trash can. "Yeah, it was. Where the hell were you?"

Matt had the grace to look uncomfortable. "My bad. I had a hot date last night. Things got carried away and I forgot to charge my phone." He stood and walked three feet and dropped into a swivel chair, leaning back and crossing his scuffed boots on the edge of his desk. Shoving the rest of the donut in his yap he reached out for the file. "Let me do a quick catch up and I'll be ready to go."

Connor bit back a sharp retort and handed over the paperwork, frowning over his partner's dark head as he bent to read. Matthew was a good man and a great partner to have watching your six, but when it came to the monotony of investigation and hours of research he bombed. The guy was hard-wired to operate at one hundred miles an hour; he didn't do slow. Why he had taken up detective work, which constituted eighty percent analysis and very little on the actual chase, O'Rourke didn't know.

"I'm going to take a trip to see our witness. You coming?" He chose not to evaluate his relief when Matt shook his head.

"If you don't need me I'll hang out here and get this done." He set his cup on the desk and sloshed. Ignoring the mess, he grabbed a pen and paper and wrote a few notes, his attention on the case. Now.

Connor brushed aside the snide thought and grabbed a paper towel, setting it under the cup. Already a coffee ring had formed, adding to the collection.

He hesitated, then shut down his computer and started for the door. "Let me know what you find." Fresh eyes might help. He was willing to take whatever he could get at this point.

The entire trip across town was spent convincing himself it was necessary to the case that he question the witness further. It had nothing at all to do with a willowy body or golden hair. He was curious about the silver streak he'd noticed earlier. Was it a dye job? And if so, why gray? In his experience women tried to make themselves look as though they drank from the fountain of youth, not the pond of wisdom.

There was a lot about Julie Crenshaw that interested him.

He found the street and drove slowly, searching for the right house number. A few kids had just finished a ball game and were straggling home, reluctant to end their fun. He remembered those days. He'd lived for baseball, even made it to college on a scholarship. But a torn ACL put an end to those dreams. He'd traded sports for police work, following in his father's footsteps to his family's dismay. "One cop in the O'Rourke clan is more than enough," his mother had cried. His dad, on the other hand, had strutted around for days like a rooster with his chest stuck out.

The house came up on his left. A nice little bungalow, white with a brightly painted red door. Good luck, if you believed that Feng Shui stuff.

He stopped behind her Civic parked in the drive, and took a moment to give himself a talking to. He was there to get information, not to ask the woman out, so quit with the sweating already. He blew out a deep breath and swung the car door open, narrowly missing the kid on the sidewalk.

"You parked on the wrong side of the street," the boy accused. He had a splattering of freckles across the bridge of his nose and hazel eyes. He'd used his jacket to make a cape, the sleeves tied around his neck, sandy hair tousled from play. He couldn't be more than six or seven going by his midget size.

"Yeah, sorry," Connor said, climbing out and towering over the would-be superhero. "This your house?"

The kid backed up a few steps and glanced nervously at his house, then at the lights on the patrol car, before lowering his chin and shooting him a worried look. "We didn't do nothin' wrong. You leave my brother alone."

The kid took off for his house before Connor could get a word in edgeways. He stared, bemused, as the boy ran up the stairs and slammed that bright red door behind him like a giant exclamation mark.

Guess he just got told.

A moment later the door opened and Julie—Mrs. Crenshaw—stepped out onto the landing, her expression matching the defiant one of her son's. He'd read up on their history before making the trip over. Husband killed a little over a year ago in a vehicle collision with bad boy movie stars, Lucas Carmichael and Scott Anderson. Carmichael and Anderson's sister never made it. And neither did the Crenshaw's unborn child. It was no wonder the remaining family carried a gravel pit worth of attitude on their shoulders.

"What are you doing here, detective?" She glided down the stairs and met him at the gate. It bothered him more than he liked to see the lines of stress between her brows. His fingers itched to massage them away. His lips ached to soothe her pain. He was so screwed.

He cleared his throat. "I have a few more questions about this morning." No need to come across pushy, O'Rourke. "If you have a minute?"

She sighed and nodded, sliding a stray hair behind her ear. He noticed she had a double piercing and wore delicate gold hoops. Wonder if she had any other piercings? His zipper jumped and he cursed under his breath.

"Pardon me?" She frowned and shifted back a step.

Smart girl.

"I just remembered I forgot to bring some papers for you to sign." He made up on the spur of the moment. "Your account of the crime scene. That's okay for now, you can stop by the department in a day or two to sign." Way to go, dumb-ass. Now she'd think he was nuts. Which he was, for coming here like this.

He pulled his notebook out of his pocket and opened to a new page, determined to get back to the case. "Can you tell me again when you first noticed the evidence?"

Julie gazed off down the street, the setting sun caught in her hair. "When we moved here I started a morning routine of running at the beach before work." She met his gaze, her eyes filled with remembered horror. "I saw something and thought a family might have left a jacket or whatever, behind. It happens quite often. Then I saw the shoe and realized there was a severed foot inside." She shivered. "I called 911 right away."

He looked at her, skeptical. "Not your news team?"

She threw her head back like a spirited thoroughbred. "No, detective. I did *not* call my team.

They must have heard it through the grapevine, it wasn't from me."

She turned and strode toward her house, stopping on the bottom stair beside a clay bowl filled with pink flowers. "Is that all? I have dinner to make for my sons."

O'Rourke closed the notepad and tapped it in his other hand. "Yes, ma'am, that's it for now. Have a nice evening."

She hesitated over a sharp nod, then climbed the remaining stairs and gently closed the red door behind her lithe body.

Some luck.

CHAPTER SIX

There she was, right on time.

He lowered the binoculars and slid his ball cap over his eyes, slouching in the cab of the truck. She wore red today, like the whore she was. The running pants were so tight he could see the outline of the thong she wore beneath. Her shirt was one of those cap sleeve affairs, with a deep v-neckline cut so that her tits were in danger of falling out as she jogged. Her hair was long and blond, just the way he liked it, brushed back from her face in a high ponytail that swished side-to-side with each step. He clenched his hand on his lap, imagining the silky strands wrapped like rope around his closed fist.

He'd noticed her a couple of weeks ago, but he'd been a might busy with his… *guest* at the time and couldn't do anything about it.

But he could now.

She was closer, running straight for him, white cords dangling from her ears, legs pumping, chest thrust forward, shoulders back. His pulse leaped in anticipation, his dick hardening in an instant. Yes, she'd do just fine.

She jogged past without even noticing him.

It pissed him off. She deserved the lesson he was going to teach her. How many times did he have to tell her…?

He shook his head, coming back to the present with a jolt. He sat up and looked through his side mirror—damn, she was already a block away. She'd been lucky this time; we'll see how long that lasts.

He watched her sweet ass until it disappeared from sight, then started the truck and listened to that diesel rattle before shifting into low and idling down the street in a puff of black smoke.

***

Julie pulled the earplugs out and glanced both ways before crossing the street at the intersection and starting the last sprint for home. She liked these early morning jogs after she got the kids off to school and tried to manage it a couple times a week. The fresh air cleared her head and let her get into the right mindset for her job. Without Taylor and the rest of the crew, she didn't know how she could have survived. They gave her a reason to get up in the morning. A way to overcome the detritus of her thoughts and focus on the lives that mattered most—her boys.

Mike hated the fact that she had to work to help out with the bills. She'd argued until she was blue in the face that she didn't mind, actually enjoyed her job, but he'd never seen it that way. His job as an electrician paid well, but with two young children, a mortgage, and a less-than-new van always in need of repair, money floated out the door. She'd started out as a researcher for the news station, but when the opportunity to train as a reporter came, she grabbed it—and thrived. She loved the adrenaline rush whenever a new story broke and it was all hands on deck. Or when they did meaningful posts that made a difference in someone's life—it felt good. Satisfying.

Even when she'd found out she was pregnant with their daughter—she closed her eyes and breathed through the pain—she'd planned to work for as long as they would let her. She'd been five months along when her nice, safe world collapsed. When she came to, her baby was gone and her husband lay crushed behind a crumbled steering wheel.

When she got home, she did a couple of stretches to loosen up after the run, then wandered into the kitchen in search of a cool drink, then headed for the shower. Time to get ready for work.

Arriving at the station a short time later, Julie was amazed all over again at the beautiful city she got to call home—even if it was temporary. A stately line of flowering cherry trees lined both sides of the street in a stunning canopy of pink highlighted by Washington's towering Cascade mountains in the distance. It was one of those perfect spring days that brought a smile to everyone's lips. The skies were a cerulean blue and a warm breeze with just a hint of ocean brine carried the tune of birds singing and people strolling. Hard to imagine just over a week ago she'd stumbled across a possible murder.

The dark corridor and coolness from the air conditioning system was oppressive after the sunshine. Julie shivered and hurried down the employee entrance, relieved when she reached the security door at the other end. She pushed the steel bar and slid into another world. One filled with chaotic order. The room, long and narrow with twenty foot ceilings and track lighting, was the hub for the VIBS broadcasting station. Line producers and editors called back and forth across the vast space while journalists and reporters filled the desks with a scramble of notes and computer printouts that would somehow develop into comprehensive reports in time for the six o'clock news.

It was crazy and exciting and she loved it.

"About time, Crenshaw. You on holidays or what?" Ron Henderson leaned back in his swivel chair, hands behind his head, hair rumpled, and tie askew.

Heat flared and she cursed her fair skin. Ron looked as though he'd pulled an all-nighter which led her to wonder what she'd missed. Not that she'd let him know that.

"Just because you don't have a life, Ron, doesn't mean the rest of us need to live and breathe the news." She ignored the inquisitive looks from nearby and strode to her desk, glancing with dismay at the pile of messages stacked near the phone.

Henderson's chair creaked as he sat up and stretched some admittedly nice looking muscles and brought her attention back to him.

"What's going on, Ron?" Curiosity won out. Julie set her bag down and picked up the memos. The first three were from Detective O'Rourke requesting her to call as soon as possible. Under that was a note from Taylor in bold letters, 'Don't Talk to Anyone.'

What the hell?

"You didn't hear?" Henderson's mouth formed a grim line. He leaned forward and turned his computer and the headline leaped out at her.

ABC Murderer Strikes Again.

CHAPTER SEVEN

Lucas leaned against a brick wall and tried to stay out of the way. Just because no one could see him, didn't mean they couldn't feel him. He'd found out the hard way when a woman stumbled through him the other day. Talk about weird. He'd seen her coming at the last minute and hadn't been able to avoid the collision. She'd pushed right through his body and stretched his skin like a balloon—then pop, she was free.

The experience shook her and freaked him out.

She'd turned seven shades of green and looked ready to hurl, while he patted himself down to make sure everything was where it was supposed to be.

After that he learned. Humans and angels don't mix.

And speaking of ghosts… Mike's wife seemed pale. She'd been trading insults with the jock at the next desk when he'd said something obviously upsetting.

Lucas straightened, ready to kick the guy's ass. She'd survived everything fate had thrown at her; she didn't need some jackass making offensive remarks. Never mind the fact fate had a name and it was Lucas.

She raised a trembling hand to her lips, and let the notes in her other hand flutter to the ground unnoticed. What was going on?

He skirted the nearby desks and sidestepped a couple of reporters in a hurry to get somewhere. When he got closer Lucas noticed the desktop computer pointed in Julie's direction. He read the headline. Who names a killer the ABC Murderer? Was he an escapee from Sesame Street out to do in the Alphabet Gang? But one glance at the shocked and stony faces in front of him and he knew this was serious.

Shit.

What was Mike's wife doing caught up in the middle of a murder investigation? How was this going to help him find Natalya? If Julie got hurt, he might never get another chance to bring the other angel out of hiding.

On the other hand, maybe he could use this somehow to draw the bastard out.

Julie sank into her chair, shrinking before his eyes. "When? What happened?" She closed her eyes and inhaled, then slowly let it out and sat up, reaching for a pen and paper. "Give me the details. This is my story."

Lucas had to give her credit; the chick had balls.

The other dude, Ron Henderson his plaque read, let out a snort and shook his head, turning the computer so she couldn't see it anymore. "I don't think so. This is the biggest case this city has seen. You're not taking all the creds."

"Don't be a jackass, Ron. We're on the same side." Julie leaned over and picked up the pieces of paper spread out around her chair like confetti. "All I meant was I already have an in with the detective on the investigation. See?" She held out a lime green post-it with O'Rourke scrawled out in a bold black slash.

Interest flared in the other man's eyes. He held his hand out. "C'mon, Crenshaw. This isn't a good time to try and prove something. You have two guppies who need their momma."

She laughed. "Guppies? You can say it, Ron—children. It's not a disease, you know."

He frowned, not impressed with her humor. "Whatever. Just let the big boys do their job. You can report on High Tea at the Empress, or something."

Julie stood and managed to stare down her nose at the still seated Henderson, even though he was damn near her height. "I'm going down to the police station for my meeting with the detective. Let me know when you manage to dig that stick out of your ass. We can compare notes and maybe help catch a killer before he finds the next victim."

A couple reporters who had been listening, whooped and clapped their hands after her speech. Instead of preening at their cheers, she gave them the shut-up-and-get-back-to-work look all mothers have mastered. They suddenly became busy with the papers on their desk, and Lucas' estimation of Mike's choice of wife climbed several notches. Not that he could let that stop what he had to do, but it wouldn't make it any easier for him either.

She lifted her head and strode past the other desks in wedge sandals and navy skirt, her cheeks flushed. Lucas tailed behind, trying to get a read on the other angel. Nothing yet. Where the hell—he grimaced at the flash of pain nailing his temples—was he? Didn't he care that his family might be in danger?

He had to hurry and slide through the door she slammed open before it closed in his face. He was still getting the hang of his new ephemeral body and wasn't sure of his capabilities. So far, the only time he seemed to have any real power was under stressful situations. Like when his best friend, Scott, was held at gunpoint by none other than their long-time agent and supposed friend, Ray Farrell.

Julie twisted her ankle hurrying down the steps. Before Lucas could react she'd straightened, glared at the sidewalk, and continued on her way. She reminded him of Scott's new girlfriend, Tracy York, the medical examiner who had processed their accident. It had taken a while for Scott to get over the loss of his sister. Tracy helped, she was good for him.

During that time, they'd found by some twist of fate, Lucas was able to communicate with his old buddy. It wasn't the same as hanging out together, but it was better than never talking to him again. He didn't know how he was going to tell Scott his sister was missing. In Heaven. Wasn't there a rule against kidnapping once you were dead?

Mike better hope nothing happened to Natalya, or all the angels in heaven weren't going to be enough to save him. Nat was… special. She hadn't asked for any of this. Lucas had been drawn to her from the moment they met as kids. She had this inner glow, it made him want to cherish and protect her from the hardscrabble life they all had growing up with parents who didn't give a shit. And then, just when she was beginning to make something of her life, he ended it in one fatal instant; a light snuffed out forever.

That was on him and he had to live with it on his conscience for the rest of eternity. Just as he had to live with the fact Mike had also died that day and lost his family. If there was a price to pay for what he'd done, he'd pay it—just let Natalya be safe.

He followed Mrs. Crenshaw to her car. He needed to distance himself from any sympathy he had for the widow so he could do what needed done. He'd tried delving into her mind but his newfound powers didn't seem work on her. There had to be a way to get Mike's attention.

Desperate times called for desperate measures. Before she could climb into the car he closed his eyes and concentrated. It was getting harder to do, but then, all of a sudden a weird tremor passed through his body like an electric current, and boom…

He stood before her in all his overweight, middle-aged taxi-man, glory. And she screamed.

CHAPTER EIGHT

A shadow of movement drew Julie out of her thoughts. She turned and her heart jumped painfully. A man followed no more than two feet behind her. Her overactive imagination painted a monster's face with clawed talons raised to swipe at her head. She screamed, her hands flapping uncontrollably. Her breathing whistled through suddenly dry lips and her tongue cleaved to the roof of her mouth.

His eyes grew wide and he backed up a couple paces. He was saying something, but she couldn't hear for the ringing in her ears. Or was that the shrieking? He'd morphed into a normal mortal who looked mortified at startling the bejesus out of her. She cut the cry off with a hand fisted against her mouth. Now that she was calming down, Julie was embarrassed. The man standing before her could be someone's grandfather. Graying hair, basketball stomach covered by a wrinkled blue t-shirt. Stubby, and slightly bowlegged, he wore carpenter pants and scuffed dress shoes and was holding her scarf in his hand.

In other words—not a monster.

"… thought you would like this back," he was saying, his eyes crinkled with concern. He glanced around, then chanced a step closer. "You okay, miss?"

No. Not really.

So much for thinking she had her emotions under control. After losing Mike and the baby she'd been in such a mess the doctors prescribed antidepressants to calm her down. There'd been moments when she'd looked at that bottle of pills and thought how easy it would be to swallow a handful and let the pain disappear. But then she'd hear either Dustin or Freddie playing in the hallway and she'd close the bottle, return it to the medicine cupboard, and avoid the mirror when she closed the door.

But that was over a year ago. Julie thought she'd overcome that dark hole inside herself. Apparently, it had just gone into hiding.

Suppressing a tired sigh, she held out her hand and forced a smile on the hapless good Samaritan. "Sorry, I didn't mean to freak you out. Bad nerves, I guess." She fingered the watered silk scarf he handed to her—a Christmas gift from Mike. "Thank you. I would've hated to lose this."

The man rubbed his grizzled jaw and shrugged uncomfortably. "'Tis no problem." He hesitated a moment, then cleared his throat. "You need to be careful, miss. There's bad people out there just waiting for the unsuspecting. Best pay attention to your surroundings."

Julie sucked in a harsh breath. Was that a warning? She looked, but there was no one nearby if she needed help. How stupid. Those dead women hadn't taught her anything?

His brows rose and he shuffled back another couple steps, hands raised in a sign of peace. "Hey, now. I don't mean you no harm. That's just a lesson I always told … a friend of mine. Not that she listened much, either. It cost her her life."

The breeze kicked up and blew Julie's long hair in front of her face, stinging her eyes and causing quick tears. At least that's the reason she told herself. The pain in the man's voice when he spoke of his friend tugged at her heartstrings. She knew that kind of agony and sympathized with his loss.

She impulsively reached out and squeezed the man's hand in sympathy, surprised at the chill in his fingers. It wasn't that cold out. Maybe he'd been ill recently? He did seem rather pale.

The detective could wait. She owed this man. A little company at a public restaurant wouldn't hurt anything. And actually, it might do some good.

Julie pointed to the little sidewalk café she regularly frequented on the next block. "Listen, want to grab a cup of coffee?"

He glanced from the restaurant to her in surprise. "You don't need to repay me, miss. I was jus' doing my duty."

Rather an odd turn of phrase. She shrugged and turned toward her car.

"Wait," he called. "I'd… I'd be happy to have coffee with ya. If you still want to, that is."

Surprised at the relief that coursed through her veins, Julie smiled and wrapped the scarf around her bunched up hair, making an impromptu ponytail, then held out her hand again. "I'm Julie Crenshaw, nice to meet you."

An indecipherable look passed through his eyes like a bank of fast moving clouds. He disregarded the handshake, instead holding out his arm in a gentleman's pose.

"Lucas. Just Lucas," he replied.

***

What the hell was Carmichael doing with his wife?

Mike hovered above the buildings, watching the two of them make their way down the street, Lucas guiding her like some portly gentleman of the eighteen hundred's. It had taken everything in him to stay back and just watch when Lucas floated out the door behind Jules and transformed into that human taxi driver form he'd been given since the accident. Mike knew Lucas was after him, but it was a new low to go after him through his wife.

The bastard.

His gaze returned to Julie. She was so damn beautiful it made his throat tighten. He missed her and the boys every moment of every day. The thought of facing eternity without them was a raw ache. Her hair had more blond to it now. Maybe because of this west coast sunshine. He squinted at the sky, almost an indigo blue. This was their dream, to live on the coast. Raise their boys to have the same love of the ocean they had gained from their honeymoon... aw, the pain. He rubbed a hand over his heart, but no amount of massaging was going to ease this agony.

All because of a fool.

As though he could sense the animosity aimed like an arrow to his back, Lucas glanced up. Mike froze, then relaxed. There was no way he could know he was there with this invisibility cloak he'd placed around himself. A neat little trick he'd learned after arriving in Heaven. One that he forgot to pass on to his partner. He still couldn't believe Father had paired them together. He had to have known it would be like adding gas to a flame.

The wind ruffled his wings, bringing him back to the present. Jules was wearing the scarf he'd gotten her for their third Christmas together, shortly after Dustin was born. He must be getting so big by now. He was what, almost nine?

Hatred for everything the man below, holding his wife by the arm, had taken from him created a sour taste in his mouth. One that seemed to grow every time he thought of the woman he held hostage. She was an innocent in this—like Jules.

But now that he'd begun this course of action, he didn't see a way to change it. Lucas needed a lesson in humility.

And he needed revenge.

CHAPTER NINE

O'Rourke stood beside his partner and listened as the medical examiner gave the time of death—approximately forty-eight hours earlier. He was waiting on test results to narrow that window further. The toxicology report stated their vic had been injected with a dose of ketamine. Abrasions and bruising of the thighs and throat suggested she'd been raped and left for dead on a forestry trunk road. They were running the DNA against known sexual predators to see if they got a hit.

Oh yeah, and her left foot had been severed at the ankle.

"Any idea how long he held her?" Matthew asked, his face betraying none of the anger and frustration they both felt. This woman had a family. People who loved and cared for her. And now, because some sick monster had caught her in his sights, all they had were memories.

"According to the ligature marks on her wrists and… ankle," he cleared his throat, "I'd say at least a week, maybe ten days."

"How soon before you can verify if the remains found last week match our victim?" Connor stared into the young woman's pale face and let the rage flow. Anger was good. It helped to block the helplessness that threatened to overwhelm him. Murder was always bad, but usually it stemmed from a crime of passion. Serial killers were different. They worked from a different plane. Cold. Methodical. Brutal.

It made his job that much tougher. Instead of being able to work through a viable list of suspects, starting with the deceased's spouse, they had to start from the inside out—so to speak. The evidence could teach them a lot about the suspect, hopefully enough to lead them to an arrest.

"Anything else, doc?" he asked, intending to spend the rest of the afternoon going through missing person reports. Her family deserved closure.

"You're going to want to see this." Doctor Robinson pushed his spectacles up his nose and turned down the edge of the white sheet draping the woman's frame on the table. "He branded her. Perimortem."

Connor sucked in a harsh breath. The bruising and rawness of the flesh surrounding the injury made it difficult to concentrate on the pattern. She'd suffered. He planned to make sure the son-of-a-bitch who did this paid.

"It looks like a puzzle piece," Matt muttered, squinting to get a better look.

The ME pulled a magnifier on a long metal arm closer to the victim's right breast. "I'd have to run more tests, but I think we'll find it was fashioned from a cattle brand."

Connor's gut burned. How could a human being treat another human this way? The short answer—a psychopath.

The burn was about an inch and a half long by an inch wide. It covered most of the underside of the woman's breast. As though he wanted it hidden, the bastard. It was definitely shaped like a puzzle piece, with an elongated raised *S* in the center, the head of a serpent forming the top of the letter.

Connor looked at his partner. They were on the same wavelength. This was something they could use. He had to have had it specially manufactured, and even if he did it himself, this kind of workmanship showed training. There couldn't be that many places that taught blacksmithing.

"Can you send us copies of this, doc?"

"Already done." The ME stepped back and wrote a memo on a clipboard attached by cord to the side of the table. "Gotta write myself notes these days or I'd forget my name," he joked.

Connor and Matthew nodded and left. Connor drew in a lungful of air, crisp and clean after a spring rain, grateful for this break they'd been afforded in the case.

"What do you think the S stands for?" Matt asked, squinting against the nebulous light from an overcast sky.

"When are you going to break down and buy some glasses?" Connor said, only half teasing.

Matt widened his green eyes and batted his lashes theatrically. "Why honey, I didn't know it mattered so much to you."

Connor shook his head, disgusted. "Seriously, buddy. I need you firing on all cylinders if we want to catch this guy. You get me?"

Matt straightened, the humor fading as though it had never been. "Like I said, *Detective*. What do you think the S stands for?"

Great. Now he'd pissed him off. If there was one thing that Connor freely admitted he sucked at, it was diplomacy. Better to let him cool down first, apologize later. Or never. Another thing he wasn't good at doing.

He scrubbed his chin and wished for a razor. They'd been putting in long hours on this, he needed to cut his partner some slack.

"Not sure. Her name? Or snake since that's what it portrayed? Maybe the name of a gang?" He shrugged. "There's too many variables yet. I think our best bet is to track down that blacksmith forge and go from there. I'm going to head back to the office and get a list started. What about you?"

"I'm thinking a trip to the tattoo parlor might be a plan. Those markings remind me of something, I'm just not sure what yet. And those guys hear a lot of shit." Matt turned toward his cruiser, a souped-up 5.7 litre Charger in steel gray. "You should stop and check in on the widow. Our guy catches wind of her, it might be a giant bulls-eye for him."

Shit. Why hadn't he thought of that? Julie was a public figure. A reporter. If their perp found out she had a tie to the case, he might decide to use her as a giant *screw you* to the police force.

He was already heading to his own sedate sedan as Matthew roared away.

CHAPTER TEN

Julie sat back and sipped her double latte, amazed by the amount of food her companion had managed to stuff himself with—and he wasn't done yet. A ginormous slice of strawberry rhubarb pie covered in thick creamy globs of French vanilla ice cream had just been served and from his expression you'd think the man had died and gone to Heaven.

Rather than watch him eat, she took in the cozy restaurant's quaint décor. Popular with the locals, the café was half-filled with four and six seater booths offering both comfort and privacy. Situated near the waterfront and the iconic Empress Hotel, the atmosphere was warm and lively. Bright yellow paint clashed with cutouts of favorite menu items displayed on the walls. A counter running the length of the narrow room showed off a vast selection of fruits and vegetables used to create their delicious plates of food.

"You sure you don't want dessert? This is the best pie I've had in a long time." The man—Lucas—brought her attention back to his nearly emptied plate. His grizzled jaw carried the evidence of his enjoyment. Julie pointed at her chin and he swiped a napkin self-consciously over the stain. "What's that saying? You can dress 'em up but you can't take them out."

She grinned, amazed by how comfortable she was in this stranger's presence. He had a look about him that reminded her of her grandfather who'd died when she was ten. He'd been a kind and loving part of her childhood, often picking her up from her parents' house for some *getaway time*, as he put it.

"Your parents need getaway time. Why don't you and me see what we can get away with, Jules?" he'd say in his gravelly voice, eyes twinkling with mischief, and a big dimple would appear in his cheek as he grinned.

The only other person to ever call her Jules had been... Mike.

"I'm sorry, did I say something wrong?" Lucas asked, his face creased with worry.

Julie shrugged off the past. "No. I'm glad you agreed to join me. It's not as much fun to coffee alone." She fingered the scarf around her neck and smiled. "Besides, I owed you a thanks for this."

He waved his fork in the air. "Like I said, it was no problem. I'm just glad I noticed it before the wind carried it away."

As if to emphasize his point, a gust of air blew the rain that had started a few minutes earlier against the plate glass window, startling her with a loud splat.

"There's only one guarantee when it comes to the weather," Lucas grinned. "It's gonna change."

Julie grimaced. He was right. Why hadn't she remembered her umbrella?

Because she'd been annoyed at the usual macho bullshit that accompanied her position and let Henderson get to her, that's why. So now she was going to go through the rest of the day with frizzy hair and damp clothes. And she still had to meet with the detective. Great.

On a scale of one to ten, this day had done a nosedive. A quick glance at the sunflower wall clock told her she'd better get a move on before Ron decided to ignore her and go after the story himself.

She reached into her purse, pulled out some cash and ignoring Lucas' protest, stuffed it under the edge of her plate, then stood and prepared to brave the elements.

"I'm sorry, but I have to get going," she said, wrapping the scarf around her head in hopes of keeping her willful hair under control. "It was nice meeting you."

Lucas twisted his bulk out of the booth, grunting a little as he rose. He swiped a few crumbs off his chest and straightened his shirt to cover his stomach before gazing at the storm lashing the windows. "You sure you want to go out in that?" he asked.

Well… no, she really didn't. But her job might be on the line, not to mention some poor woman's life,

so she would do what she needed to, elements be
damned.

"I'll be fine. Though my grandpa always said
water weakens you." She smiled and moved toward
the door. Maybe if she ran to her car she wouldn't get
soaked.

"Why don't you let me drive you where you want
to go?"

Lucas' voice stopped her in her tracks. She turned
and met his beseeching gaze.

"C'mon. You can't turn down my gentlemanly
offer." Julie started to shake her head and he hurried
to add, "I drive taxi for a livin', it won't mean a
thing."

She laughed off her discomfort. For a moment
he'd seemed desperate to keep her with him. Silly, of
course. This case must be getting to her more than she
thought.

"I don't want to send you into this rain if you're on
your break, Mr..... Lucas," she said, awkwardly.

He brushed past and opened the door. A blast of
cold rain preceded his words, "Wait here, I'll be right

back." He hurried down the steps, gray head bent against the driving rain, and disappeared into the growing fog.

One thing Julie had learned about island life, being near the water meant dealing with swift changes in weather patterns. Mike had always loved the rain. It was one of the reasons he'd wanted to move here. The lushness of the rainforest, giant cedars, and the lure of the ocean called to both of them. They'd planned to raise their family in this ecological wonder of the world, but he'd died before they got the chance.

A yellow cab sporting a black stripe and resembling a motorized bumble bee pulled up to the curb. Julie bundled her wool jacket, pushed the door open, and hurried down the stairs, grateful for the kindness of a stranger. As she settled in the front seat, warm air wafted through the center vents, sending a gold cross hanging off the mirror twirling crazily.

"Where to?" Lucas asked, glancing over while shifting the car into gear.

Startled, she looked up from the hypnotic swaying of the religious symbol. "Oh, the police station, please."

Now it was his turn to look alarmed. "You in trouble?"

She smiled, charmed by his obvious concern. "No, I'm not in trouble. I have a meeting with one of the detectives. I'm a reporter."

The rain decided to kick it up a notch and Lucas switched the wipers to high and the vents to defrost. Julie was relieved to see him slow down and place both hands on the wheel. There wasn't a lot of traffic moving around in this weather, but she couldn't help tensing anyway. She was well aware of how quick accidents occur. A blink of an eye and your whole world could change.

"A reporter, huh?" Lucas' voice drew her back, grounding her in the now, instead of then. "What made you choose that for a career? It's not the friendliest profession, is it? Those microphones and cameras up in a person's business until you're ready to punch someone's lights out." He glanced her way, his gaze hooded. "No offence."

Her curiosity piqued, Julie turned in her seat and searched his suddenly grim countenance. "You don't like reporters much by the sound of it."

"Does anyone like people nosing into their business?" He tried to laugh it off, but she wasn't buying it.

"What happened, Lucas?"

He shrugged. "I didn't always drive cabs for a livin', that's all." He shot her a swift look from unfathomable eyes. "We all have secrets; things we wish we could change. Even you, I bet."

Especially her.

Julie faced forward and stared at the mesmerizing effect of the rain slanting against the windshield through the tears blurring her vision.

CHAPTER ELEVEN

Connor spent a frustrating couple of hours chasing the shadow that was Julie Crenshaw. The news station turned out to be his first big mistake. Those bloodhounds never knew how to leave well enough alone. The second he'd given his name at the door, he'd been guided right inside. Clenching his gut to smother the annoying butterflies—probably heartburn from the burrito he'd wolfed down for breakfast—he rubbed his pec a couple times and followed a woman in corduroy coveralls down the hall.

"Aren't you that detective who upset Julie at the beach last week?" She glanced over her shoulder and gave him the once-over. The look in her eye said she found him lacking.

"I'm pretty sure she was distraught before I arrived," he said, noncommittedly. *How long was this hallway?*

They sidestepped around a scissor-lift parked against the wall and the door came into view. He let out a near silent sigh of relief that turned out to be premature because she turned and held up a hand, halting their progress.

"Listen, I get that you have a job to do, we all do, but Julie is different. She's been through some bad shit, so take it easy on her, okay?" Striking blue eyes zapped him with laser-beam intensity. He'd been warned.

If he weren't so anxious to make sure Crenshaw was safe, he'd have found this little exchange amusing. Connor was glad she had people in her corner, it must be tough juggling a full-time job and both parenting roles to a couple of growing boys.

The thought of her struggling to get by after losing her husband twisted the tension in his stomach another notch. Though why it should matter to him that she'd once been a happily married woman, he didn't care to guess.

"I just have a few questions," he said to the firecracker bristling before him. "I'm not here to cause trouble."

"Well, see that you don't," she huffed, then spun on her heel and slapped the crossbar on the door, allowing it to open with a crash loud enough to wake the dead.

Several sets of eyes centered on him like he was a bullseye and they held the darts. Friendly bunch.

He followed Julie's champion down a row of mix-and-match desks, some occupied, some recently vacated if the mess of papers and flickering computer screens were anything to go by.

She slowed near an empty desk crowded with different-sized framed pictures, stacks of folders, and maybe the largest red coffee mug he'd ever seen.

"Ron, where is Julie?" The woman stood, hands on trim hips, and glared at the surly looking hulk leaning back in his seat, feet crossed on the edge of a scarred wooden desk.

"Do I look like her mother?" he scowled. "What do you want from me, Sam?" He dropped his legs, but remained seated, his dark gaze landing on Connor. "Who the hell is this?"

Connor stepped forward, angling between the combatants. "Detective O'Rourke. Mind answering a few questions…?" This guy was carrying a serious chip on his shoulder. Connor was tempted to knock it off. He didn't like men who spoke offensively to women. It reminded him of his childhood a little too much for comfort.

The guy finally got to his feet. He was big, three or four inches over Connor's own six feet. With linebacker shoulders and visible ink, he cut an intimidating figure. Not that Sam seemed very alarmed.

"That's Ron Henderson. He's *supposed* to be helping Julie learn the ropes," she said, sarcasm ripe in her voice.

"I can talk for myself, thank you. Don't you have a truck to clean or something?" He kicked his chair out of the way and strolled around the corner of his desk.

She shot him a go to hell look and touched Connor's arm. "His bark is almost as bad as his bite. Don't get too close and you'll be fine." Satisfied she'd gotten the last word in, Sam grinned and sauntered down the rest of the row and out of sight.

Ron shook his head and turned to Connor. "What do you want to know, detective?"

"How long have you been a reporter, Henderson?" The man had the look of a jaded cop. Eyes that had seen too much, a mouth that had lost the ability to smile naturally. Tough, leathery skin. A lot like himself. Connor rubbed his pec again.

Henderson stood taller. "What difference does that make?"

"I just wanted to know how qualified you are. Telling the news is a big responsibility." Connor quit prevaricating and made his point. "You don't want to be jumping any guns and creating a mass hysteria with the public. I think Julie... Mrs. Crenshaw, could be in over her head. If it's your job to take care of her, I suggest you do it. Get her off this case before she gets hurt."

Fuck, stick to business shithead.

Henderson's ears perked up at the personal reference. He relaxed and leaned against the desk, boots crossed at the ankle, hands cupping the edge of the desk on either side of his jean-clad hips. "She's right pretty, ain't she, *detective.* Maybe you're a touch more invested in her than the case. "

Connor's hands fisted and of course Henderson picked up on the tell. His lips quirked. "Julie is her own person, O'Rourke. I've already tried to talk her out of following this story, but she's sunk her teeth into it. All *I* can do now is watch her back, and keep her as safe as possible. Meanwhile, if you quit harassing the news media, do *your* job and catch this motherfucker, we won't need to worry about our girl anymore. Right, Detective?"

How the hell had he managed to lose control of this conversation? And who decided she was *our girl*? Julie Crenshaw was no one's girl. She was all woman.

CHAPTER TWELVE

Mike followed the taxi carrying his wife through the fog and rain. What was Lucas doing? He should be freaking out at the disappearance of his—whatever she was to him. Not down here messing around with Mike's wife.

Even if it was just as a cab-driver.

Why was he bothering? What did he want?

Jules couldn't help him find the girl. None of this made sense. Then again, it didn't make much sense to hole someone up in a cave for months just to make a point, either. He'd gone off the deep end for a while after his return to earth and the family he'd lost. Revenge dug vicious talons into his chest that hadn't eased until after he'd taken Lucas' girl.

An eye for an eye.

Except it hadn't helped, not really. He was still dead, and his wife and kids were still alone. On top of that, he liked Natalya. She had to be scared. Had to wonder what he was going to do with her. If he planned on... hurting her.

She couldn't know that he wasn't like that. His only goal at the time had been payback for what Lucas had done to him. So middle grade, when he thought of it that way. But it had bugged the shit out of him the way the guy seemed to have lived a blessed life—who wouldn't want to be a movie star?—then he dies and still gets the girl. Such bullshit.

The rain pelted his skin, but Mike didn't mind. It was infinitely preferable to the gray nothingness above. He loathed that place. Couldn't imagine spending the rest of eternity there.

Alone.

He missed Julie with every beat of his wings. Every breath he took reminded him of all he'd lost. Their daughter would have been walking by now, had she lived. He thought of her often. Wondered which of them she would have favored; Jules with her expressive hazel eyes and quicksilver temperament, or him with his dark hair and green eyes? In any case, she would have been loved ferociously. He'd been surprised, and a little hurt, when Julie decided to make the move from Chicago to Vancouver Island. It had been their dream, somehow it seemed wrong that she was continuing without him.

And yes, that made him a selfish, self-centered prick, but that's how he felt. It was bad enough he had to watch his kids grow into fine young men without his guidance, but it felt like another blow to the gut that it was happening in their dream spot and he wasn't there to enjoy it.

The cab's signal light came on and it made the turn into police headquarters. What was going on? Was Jules in trouble? His kids?

Mike dropped out of the sky like a lodestone, drawn to the flashing beacon of the taillight. He stood near the rear bumper, his wings folding against his back, and watched through the quickly fogging windows as Julie spoke to the cab driver—Lucas.

She opened the door and climbed out, her shapely legs getting splattered by the rain.

"Thank you for the ride," she said, bending over to look at the driver. "Are you sure you don't want any payment?"

Mike heard a few mumbled words from within the vehicle, then Julie said a hurried good-bye, slammed the door and raced for the covered portico, quickly disappearing from view.

Mike hesitated, torn between following his wife to find out what was going on, and confronting Lucas.

The choice was taken out of his hands when the car was thrown into park and shut off. The other angel clambered out of the vehicle and glared at him across the roof.

"Where's Natalya?" he growled.

Mike's lips twisted. "What, no hello?"

Lucas practically levitated, except his overweight human body limited his movement. His face grew florid with the effort of controlling his temper. It was quite entertaining.

He squelched through the puddles and came around to the passenger side, facing Mike with closed fists the size of ham hocks. "Where is she, you asshole? She had nothing to do with the accident. Let her go, Monk."

It was Mike's turn to growl. He hated that name. Ever since they were paired together in Heaven with the task of saving human lives in exchange for a second chance, the damn angel had given him that stupid moniker. All it did was remind him he wasn't likely to be having sex any time in the conceivable future. Something guaran-damn-teed to piss him off.

Not feeling any warm fuzzies at their reunion, Mike crossed his arms and leaned against the car. "She's safe. For now. Tell me what you're doing here, Lucas. Why are you following my wife? She can't help you find your girl, if that's what you're after."

He could see it in the other man's face, that's exactly what he was up to. Dumb angel.

But then a sly look entered Lucas' eyes. "She sure is pretty. Bet you wish you could slip into a human's body like I can, don't ya?" He rubbed Neanderthal knuckles up and down his impressive paunch. "Don't worry, I'll take care of her for you." His teeth gleamed through the drizzling rain.

Mike had him nailed to the car like a bug to a board before the last word dripped from his annoying tongue. "Shut the hell up before I…"

Lucas leaned forward, got in his face. "Before you what? Kill me? You're a little too late for that, *buddy.*"

Mike tightened his grip, tempted to slam the guy into next week. But then he saw the underlying pain in Lucas' gaze, and let him go, took a couple steps back, and watched him wrestle his shirt into submission. "Why did you bring Julie to a police station?" he asked again, calmer this time.

"She's a witness in a murder investigation."

Mike's heart leapt into his throat. "What?" He started for the doors, pushing the angel aside.

Lucas held up his hand and halted his progress. "Wait, she's fine. She saw some evidence of a crime, that's all. They just want information from her, that's why she's here."

Holy. Hell.

***

The color leeched out of the other man's already pale face and Lucas hurried to open his car door before grabbing Mike's limp arm and leading him to the seat. He'd forgotten how attached the angel was to his wife. He hadn't meant to shock him like that. Even if he did deserve it.

"Look, I'm sorry. I shouldn't have freaked you out. There's a couple of good cops on the case, and I'm here to watch her. Nothing's going to happen, okay?"

Mike swallowed hard and nodded. "What did she see?"

"It's more like what she found," Lucas said, and grabbed a stray bottle of water from the floor. "Here, drink this." He cleaned the mouth with the edge of his shirt and handed it over.

Mike grimaced, but accepted the drink. He took a deep guzzle, then swiped his mouth. "Tell me, man. I'm imagining the worst here."

"I should leave you hanging, you'd deserve it after the stunt you pulled, but one of us has to be the bigger angel." Lucas grinned and patted his gut. "And I don't mean this."

Mike growled and put a hand on either side of the door to propel himself at Lucas.

Lucas threw out his bear-paw-sized mitt and shoved the man down. "Take it easy. She found a severed foot on the beach. The cops got her statement and now they're following up. Like I said, she's fine."

The rain slithered down the nape of his neck as though to cool his temper. Beating the shit out of the guy holding his girl… friend wouldn't do anything to bring her back.

He stepped back, giving them both a little breathing space. "I know you must be worried about your ex, but she's in good hands. The detective on the case seems like a smart man, he'll look out for her."

A couple of uniforms came out the front door, eyed the cab, then continued down the steps and into the parking lot.

"I gotta get going before I get pulled over. Not sure, but I don't think it's legal to inhabit someone's body," he joked. "Why don't you tell me where I can find Nat and I'll be on my way."

Mike stood—towering over Lucas, which he hated. "Don't ever call my *wife* an ex or I'll make sure you never see the girl again."

He shoved past Lucas, his wings unfurling into a dark gray cloud as he went. Within seconds he was several feet off the ground.

Frantic, Lucas tried to shift, but couldn't seem to make the change. Mike was rising fast, soon he'd be gone from sight.

"Where is she, you son-of-a-bitch?" he shouted.

Mike turned and gazed down on him. "Keep my wife safe, angel, or you'll never find out." Then he turned, and disappeared into the mist.

CHAPTER THIRTEEN

Julie entered the police station and was hit by a case of nerves. It had been a week since she'd spoken to Detective O'Rourke, but he'd never been far from her thoughts. He made her uncomfortable—like her favorite pair of skinny jeans that just never fit the same after her pregnancy. She went on the defensive every time he was near, as though sensing danger. Which was silly. He couldn't hurt her; he didn't even know her. Not really.

She thought of her life in two parts, before the accident—and after. The person she'd been before was gone, she was changed. Tougher. Cynical. A pessimist where she'd always been an optimist. But that's okay, learn to expect the worst and you couldn't be disappointed, that was her new motto.

An officer stepped up to the window separating the public from the back. "Can I help you?"

Julie worried the strap of her bag hanging from her shoulder. "I have a meeting with Detective O'Rourke," she said.

"Name?" the female Mountie inquired.

Julie. Julie Crenshaw."

The officer looked her over with sharp eyes that didn't miss a thing. "Have a seat and I'll check if he's in." She pointed toward a row of chairs near the entry.

Julie nodded, grateful to have a moment to marshal her thoughts before the appointment. She searched her purse until she found the stick of gum Freddy had offered her last night. Usually it helped when she was anxious, she hoped it worked today. Not that she had a reason to be nervous, she hadn't done anything wrong. And if seeing Connor O'Rourke again ramped up her heartbeat and made her hands sweaty, it was only to be expected. He was a criminal investigator on the trail of a possible homicide. It had nothing at all to do with his lean body, smoky gray eyes, or copper hair with that distracting curl on the forehead.

Julie glanced down and realized she'd been twirling her wedding ring round and round on her finger. Grimacing, she stopped and ran a hand through her frizzing hair. Darn rain. Her friends had gently nudged her, hinting it was time to let the past go, maybe even date again. And maybe she would—just not yet.

Mike had been in her life for so long, she wasn't sure she could move on. He'd been her first boyfriend back when they'd been sixteen and too young to know what they wanted in life. They'd broken up and got back together all through high school, then she'd gotten pregnant with Dustin and their future was set. Not that she regretted anything. Mike was a decent man, a good provider. He'd loved becoming a father.

"He'll see you now."

Julie jumped, refocusing on the Mountie waiting to let her into the back. She gathered her belongings, then hurried to follow the woman, the steel door clanging shut behind her. There was a grouping of six or eight desks, most filled by officers either on the phone or their computers. Not so different from her job. A narrow hall, the walls painted off-white, led past a couple of rooms with closed doors—interrogation, maybe?—and ended at a conference room, the door half open as though awaiting their arrival.

The officer knocked once. A deep voice Julie remembered in her dreams bade them to enter. The Mountie smiled her reassurance, moved aside to let Julie in, then closed the door behind her. She was alone. With O'Rourke.

***

Connor smiled his thanks to Madeline and watched Julie enter the room. He should be thinking of her as Mrs. Crenshaw. He knew he needed to keep his distance, but something about her called to him on an elemental level he couldn't control. It wasn't just her looks, though she was beautiful with those high breasts, and eyes that reminded him of an autumn forest, all shadowy golds and browns. They made him want to slay dragons for her, those eyes.

"Hi." Witty, that was him. "Come in, have a seat."

She smiled uncertainly and chose a chair halfway down the conference table. Telling. Maybe he disturbed her too—the thought heated his skin and made his pulse jump.

He loosened his tie and undid the top button on his dress shirt, hesitating when she tugged her purse in front of her body. He cleared his throat. "I, ah, paid a visit to your station today. I hoped to catch you there and save you the trip." And he'd needed to see her again, not that he could tell her that.

"What's so important? Did you get a lead? Have you caught him? Who is he?" The words tumbled out like a runaway train. She reached into that suitcase she called a purse, impatiently tucked her hair behind her ear, and pulled out a digital recorder. "Mind if I use this?" she asked, holding it up for him to see.

"Hold on," he said, his hand firm on the file in front of him. "That's not why I asked you down here." Her face fell and he felt a stab of sympathy. He knew this was her first big story since moving to the island. She had something to prove, maybe more to herself than anyone else.

He rose and moved down the table, sinking into the seat next to hers. He wrapped his hand around hers holding that blasted recorder and tried to keep his mind off the fact her skin was soft as silk. He had no problem picturing it on his body, skimming, sliding, stroking. Great, now he had a hard-on to deal with.

Time to get his head in the game before he did something he'd regret, like laying her out on the conference room table.

"Jules…"

She looked up at him with shock, her skin turning pale.

"What? What did I do?" He squeezed her fingers, icy in his grip. "Talk to me, honey. I want to help."

She gazed at him blankly, then tugged her hand free. "Don't ca… call me that. I don't want you to call me that."

Jesus, way to go, Romeo. Obviously the name was special to her. Maybe her husband had used it—and there was no way he was going to contemplate when. He'd never considered himself a jealous man before, but when it came to Jules… Julie, he had that green-eyed little bugger stomping up and down screaming to be heard.

"Sure, no problem," he said. "Look, let's start again. I arranged to meet because I need to ask a couple of questions. Are you okay to answer them now?"

She glared and he was glad to see her snap back. "Of course. What is it, detective?"

Ouch, that hurt.

"Did you notice anything odd, besides your findings, on the beach that morning? Anyone who didn't quite belong? A vehicle maybe?" She shook her head and he leaned forward, desperate for any crumb she could give him. "Think, Mrs. Crenshaw. Sometimes our subconscious picks up on things we don't always notice. Try." He hesitated. "Please."

Julie opened her mouth, no doubt ready to tell him off, then a dark shadow passed over her expression. She licked her lips—he cursed himself for noticing—gave a short nod, and closed her eyes as though to concentrate.

Connor waited with bated breath, amazed at the delicate tracery of sandy lashes against peaches and cream skin. When her lids opened and she gazed at him with mysterious golden eyes a moment later he felt a sharp tug in his groin. He reached up and ran a gentle hand down that beguiling silver streak in her hair, smiling a little when she leaned into the touch.

"I'm sorry, honey. I wish…" There were a hundred things he wished, not least that he had met her at another time, another place.

She turned into his hand and placed a butterfly kiss on his palm, so fleeting he wasn't sure she'd touched him, except for the tingle she left behind. And the fact that his heart was about to explode.

"It's okay, I understand." She played with the strap on her handbag. "I don't remember seeing anyone, but there was a delivery truck parked parallel to the water. One of those big tractor-trailer units. I thought it was weird, but figured whoever it was probably needed to rest." She looked at him and the suppressed fear ripped him apart. "Was that him, Connor? Was that the killer?"

He didn't know, but he sure as hell hoped not. The driver would have had a clear vision of her walking down that beach.

CHAPTER FOURTEEN

Julie's stomach churned. What if the killer had been on the beach? He could have followed her home, seen where she lived. Watched her greet her boys after school.

God, her boys.

She pushed her chair back, the screech of the legs on the ceramic tile echoing the shriek of her nerves.

"I have to go. My boys…"

"Wait." Connor stood and reached for her hand, then let it drop to his side without touching her.

She felt the loss and tried not to think about her still tingling lips. What was she doing? Kissing a stranger's palm like some kind of… of floosy. She needed to pull herself together. Concentrate on her family. Keep them safe.

He looked around and reached for his jacket resting on an adjacent chair. "I'll come with you."

"No." She cringed, hysteria edging her tone. "They aren't even home from school yet. I'll call if there's a problem."

The last thing she needed was to explain to Dustin why the police officer was at their house—again.

She edged toward the door, anxious to leave, but pulled up short when she remembered her car was back at the newsroom. Damn.

"What's wrong?" Connor had thrown his coat on and followed her. His arm brushed her shoulder as he held the door handle and she shivered. He looked down at her and must have recognized her body's inappropriate response because he sucked in a quick breath and his eyes darkened to match the stormy gray clouds outside.

"Julie." He moved to kiss her, and God forgive her, she couldn't help it, she wanted him to. Her hands went to his chest, whether to hold him back or draw him close, she couldn't say. His head lowered— and a door clanged down the hall.

Julie jumped back as though scalded.

They were in a police station for crying-out-loud. What was she thinking?

"I gotta go. Can I wait inside the entry until a cab comes?"

He scrubbed the back of his neck, his eyes contrite. "Of course. Where is your car? Is there something wrong with it?"

She smiled, relieved to be back on neutral ground. "My baby might not be so pretty anymore, but she's as reliable as they come." Mike had always sworn by Honda. It was an easy decision to buy the old girl when they arrived on the island. The price was right, and it reminded her of their first car. "A cabdriver found my scarf earlier so I bought him a coffee and he returned the favor by driving me here during the storm." She shrugged, not sure now why she'd agreed to such a thing. She certainly could have driven herself, and not been left in this position.

Connor was frowning. She could practically see his mental gears turning and coming up with a worst case scenario. And if she'd known what she knew now, she might have thought that too. But the old cabbie had been harmless. Just a nice man out to do a good deed. She couldn't very well go around all paranoid every time someone came near her. That was crazy. She had a job that involved meeting and mingling with strangers. It's what she did and she was damn fine at it. It was unlikely that a serial killer would bother with her anyway, right?

She shivered.

"I'm sure you don't need me to tell you to be careful. You shouldn't be traveling around by yourself until this guy is caught. If he has been near a television, he'll have heard about you by now." Connor tipped her chin and stared down at her with worried eyes. "Your children need their mother. Please tell me you won't take needless risks, especially while chasing this story."

Julie's pulse skipped. His fingertips were calloused and warm where they touched her skin. It was all too easy to picture them sliding down her neck and over her suddenly aching breasts. His breath smelled faintly of the coffee he'd been drinking when she arrived. If she lifted her mouth just slightly she could taste him and find out if he liked sugar as much as she did.

His gaze changed, registering her need. His lids drooped and focused on her lips. His nostrils flared, breathing her want. She bit the inside of her lip, holding back the moan threatening to escape. She'd never been this turned on by a simple look.

His mouth lowered and found the spot she'd injured. His tongue soothed. Her heart stopped.

Waiting.

Wanting.

Aching.

He murmured something, the buzzing in her ears blocked the words. It didn't matter anymore. All she could think about was his mouth on hers.

And then it was.

***

Matt stood by impatiently waiting for Marko to finish inking a butterfly onto the shoulder of a kid young enough to be his daughter. He'd better have gotten a consent form from her parents or Matt would run him in. Kids these days. They couldn't wait to grow up and taste life's excesses. He could have told her to slow down, enjoy her youth. Once gone it was damn hard to get it back. He knew.

Marko had built up quite the clientele in the years since getting out of prison. His business, *Let It Bleed*, was popular with the young and hip as well as some… shall we say, darker, clients. It was the second category Matt was interested in.

He stood before a wall filled with a wide variety of drawings, all stapled together like some sort of decoupage gone crazy. He actually liked a couple of the designs. One in particular, had a set of angel wings in three dimensional detail spread across a stencil of a man's back. It was probably as close to Heaven as he'd ever get.

The tinkle of the bell above the door turned his attention to a heavy-set guy wearing a faded Red Sox ball cap low over his eyes. He took two steps into the store, saw Matt, and headed the other way.

Matt raced after him, ignoring Marko's, "Hey, man, not in my store."

The guy was quicker on his feet than he expected. He was already halfway across the parking lot when Matt exited the building.

"Hey, Stop. Police. I want a word with you."

The ball cap glanced back, then picked up the pace, dodging cars and a truck who'd just pulled into the lot, to duck around the side of the building, disappearing behind a dumpster.

Great, and Matt was wearing his favorite loafers.

He slowed as he came up to the garbage can, his hand resting on his firearm and heart pounding out a *don't go in there* message he was probably going to wish he'd listened to.

The wind rustled a bag and sent it tumbling along the ground, almost giving him a heart attack. There was no sign of the suspect. Where the hell was he?

Suddenly, an arm shot out and caught him square in the chin, sending him backward to land hard on his ass. He shook his head to clear the cobwebs and took a boot to the ribs.

Fuck.

What was this guy's problem?

"Police. Freeze," he panted, hand cradling his side. Left with no other choice, he pulled his service revolver and took aim on his assailant.

The guy froze and slowly lifted his hands behind his head.

Matt squinted, trying to get a good look now that he had the situation controlled, but the sun was directly in his face.

Which is why he didn't see the missile that slammed into his forehead and put him out for the count.

CHAPTER FIFTEEN

Butterflies happy-danced in Connor's chest. He held a warm, willing woman, and his lips were busy filling in the gaps between his imagination and the reality that was Julie Crenshaw.

Her skin was the softest silk. She tasted of apple pie and homemade bread. Of lazy Sunday mornings and tussled sheets.

Of home.

When she opened her eyes, they were just as bemused as his must be, but it was the slightly dazed arousal glinting out of their depths that almost sent him back for more.

"So… that happened." His mouth quirked. He eased back but retained his hold on her waist. The confusion and guilt seeping into her face disappointed him. *Her husband's only been gone a year, what did you expect?*

Connor dropped his arms and stepped back. "I'm sorry. I never meant to make you uncomfortable." He scrubbed a hand through his hair and eyed her warily.

She straightened her shirt, tucking it back into the top of her skirt with trembling fingers. He couldn't remember the last time he'd lost control like that. What the hell was wrong with him?

The buzz of his cell startled him. He tugged it out of his pocket and glanced at the screen. Great, now what?

"O'Rourke."

Julie jumped, her gaze wide-eyed as it landed on the phone in his hand.

"Detective O'Rourke? We have your name on file as first to be called in case of emergency." The preppy female's voice hesitated. "Sir, it's your partner, sir. He was brought into emergency with blunt force head trauma. Can you come?"

Connor stared at Julie, his mind blank. "What happened? Is he all right? Which hospital?"

Julie's warm honey gaze turned sympathetic. She placed a reassuring hand on his arm and squeezed.

"I can't divulge that information over the phone, sir. He's at the Jubilee. Do you know where the emergency entrance is?"

Connor opened the conference room door and waited for Julie to precede him. "Yeah, I know it. I'll be there soon, thanks." He ended the call and shoved the cellphone back into the pocket of his pants. Damn. He didn't always get along with Matt, but that didn't mean he wished the guy ill.

"I'm sorry about your friend." Julie glanced over her shoulder.

"Thanks." His smile felt flat. "He's a good cop." It was a chance they all took. The role of a police officer was filled with highs and lows. From the break that might lead to the location of a missing child and the joy of reuniting them with their frantic families, to the sometimes devastating deaths humans inflicted on one another. It was a difficult and sometimes thankless job, but the rewards outweighed the negative. Most of the time.

They were nearing the bullpen now, he could hear the muted chatter of his workmates going about their daily routines, filling out the never-ending files, making calls, doing online searches. Much of the legwork was spent with their butts planted in front of computers, different from the way television liked to portray them.

He grasped Julie's forearm, halting her momentum. She turned and looked up at him and just like that the awareness returned.

Connor cleared his throat. "Listen, about before…"

An adorable wrinkle formed between her brows. One he wished he could soothe away with his lips.

"It was a mistake."

His turn to frown now.

"Let's agree it was an aberration, shall we?" She shrugged free of his grip, her focus somewhere in the region of his neck. "Your friend needs you, you better go."

He hesitated, loathe to leave without talking it out. But really, what could he say? She lit him up like a neon sign, but she didn't strike him as a hook-up-for-a night kind of girl. And he definitely wasn't a good relationship bet, so they were at an impasse.

He nodded. She was right. "Madeline will see that you get back to your car—safely." He couldn't help it, he reached out and ran gentle fingers down the silver streak in her hair. "We'll talk later, okay?"

Madeline stepped into view and he dropped his hand. "Maddie, can you see that Mrs. Crenshaw gets a ride back to wherever her car was left?"

Maddie's glance roved between them, an indecipherable look on her pretty face. "Sure. Follow me, *Mrs*. Crenshaw."

Connor winced, even though he'd just used her married name himself. It sounded... illicit from another's lips. "Have whoever it is follow her home and set up a surveillance while you're at it."

Julie gasped. "Are you kidding me? I can't have a police escort. You're going to get me fired."

Frustrated and anxious to leave, Connor snapped the command, "That's an order, Madeline. This is an important witness to the beach murder investigation. I want her watched."

He stomped past, ignoring the knowing smirk from his officer, and the outraged anger on the face of the woman he was coming to care about.

***

Matt woke with a splitting headache and aching ribs. He needed to quit drinking, that shit was going to kill him one day. He opened his eyes to check the time and immediately slammed them shut on a groan.

Fuck, who turned on the lights?

"Wake up, Sleeping Beauty, and I ain't kissing that puss." Connor's voice reverberated in his eardrums like his father's used to after a night out carousing.

"Turn down the dial, man. Can't you see I'm wounded?"

"Probably looking for a sympathetic nurse."

Nurse? Matt forced his eyes open again, this time making sure he kept to a squint. What the hell? He was lying in a hospital bed, not his California king at home.

"What happened?" he croaked, searching until he found Connor seated on a lumpy looking armchair near the room's only window. Thank God the curtains were pulled.

Connor stood and came to his side. "I was hoping you could tell me," he said, empathy turning his eyes gunmetal gray.

Shit, was he that bad off?

He tried to sit, but the pain knocked him flat on his back again. His stomach heaved and his vision turned spotty. Son-of-a-bitch, that hurt.

Connor brought a straw in a plastic cup filled with ice chips to his lips. Grateful he took a long, slow drink, the coolness flushing away the ache.

"Thanks, man." His head fell against the stiff pillows. "How long have I been out?"

"Not sure. They brought you in a couple hours ago. Doc says you have a concussion and a couple of cracked ribs. You got lucky."

Luck.

He'd quit counting on that nebulous blessing way back in seventh grade when his pops found out he'd skipped class and taught him the hard way not to do it again.

"What happened, Matt?"

It was coming to him in a series of wavy images, like a reflection on water. "I went to the tattoo place I told you about." He remembered the sketches. "I was thinking of getting some angel wings."

Connor gave him a confused look. "Ookay, but what does that have to do with the investigation? Focus, buddy."

Matt grinned, even though it hurt his head. Some things never changed. His partner of three years was a great guy, but he had a serious lack of humor. Matt had made it his personal quest to loosen the dude up.

"I was waiting for my source to finish up a job and this guy walks in. He sees me and makes a run for it." He lifted a bandaged hand to the goose egg on his head. "He blindsided me."

"Did you get a look at him?" Connor pulled a black notebook and pen out of his pocket, ever the cop.

"Just vague things. Heavyset, maybe mid-thirty's. He had a Red Sox hat, red with black brim." He tried to visualize his attacker, but everything remained grainy, distorted. "That's it, other than he packed a hell of a wallop."

Frustrated, he turned his head and stared at the curtained window. There was silence, then Connor patted his blanket-covered leg. "Don't worry. We'll find him."

Matt's throat closed. He'd screwed up. They both knew it. Maybe he'd even let a killer get away. And that was something he had to live with.

CHAPTER SIXTEEN

Mike sank into the chair his wife had recently vacated in the conference room at the police station. He stared at the door and pictured the cop holding Jules pressed up against its smooth surface while he locked lips with her like she was in need of CPR.

And she'd let him.

His head fell back and he closed his eyes, desperately trying to erase the preceding minutes from existence. Moisture leaked down his cheeks and into his ears. The heart that he'd thought was frozen in time, cracked. Great fissures of agony and sorrow spilled into his chest, filling his soul with darkness and rage.

Why was this happening to him? Why was he being tortured this way? Wasn't it enough that he'd lost his family and then was given the task of teaching his enemy repentance? How was he supposed to stand by and watch the love of his life move on with another man? Maybe even raise his children?

No.

Mike erupted from his seat and the chair flew against the wall before bouncing to the floor. He strode for the door, determined to bust the cop's face and then grab his wife, throw her over his shoulder, and head for home where she belonged. Then the memory of what he was drew him up short. A freaking angel.

It didn't matter how much he ached to stake his claim, it wouldn't do any good, would it? Unless they were going to reenact that sappy chick flick Jules used to pick every other month for their date night, it wasn't going to work. He was a ghost—and she wasn't.

His stomach sank. That meant he was going to have to learn to accept other men entering her life, and maybe even staying.

She deserved happiness.

He blinked hard, pushing back the tears. His kids did too. Someone to take them to baseball practices. To teach them to drive, and how to treat their girlfriends right. To bounce their babies on his knee. So many experiences Mike had looked forward to sharing with Julie, but now he would be forced to watch from the sidelines. He didn't know how he was going to do it.

The door opened and a woman rushed into the room. She looked around, spotted the overturned chair, and shook her head. "How the heck…?"

The aroma of corned beef and mustard followed her across the room, and Mike inhaled. He'd loved Rueben sandwiches.

She reset the chair on its feet, grazed her fingers down the marred wall, and turned to leave, her brow creased in confusion. Something made her stop. A nervous hand went to her sidearm and she stared right at him, though Mike knew she couldn't be seeing anything.

"Who's there?" she asked, her voice only slightly tremulous. She had guts, this one.

He stood absolutely still, barely breathing.

"This isn't funny," she said.

No, it certainly wasn't.

He turned to leave and froze at the distinct sound of a safety being flipped.

"I don't know who you are, mister, or what kind of game you're playing, but you don't belong in here."

Holy shit, she could see him.

He slowly raised his hands, careful not to make any sudden moves—though really, what could she do, kill him?—and twisted at the waist to see if she was actually speaking to him. Yep, she was. She had her revolver held firm in both hands and pointed right at his body mass.

Did he say *holy shit?*

"Relax, officer, I'm not here to hurt anyone." Well, maybe the cop who'd kissed his wife. He still wasn't quite ready to accept that yet. "I can explain." *Sort of.*

"How did you get into the building? I never cleared you, and what's with the hocus pocus crap?"

He started to let his hands drop and she waved them up again. "Not so fast, buddy. You have some explaining to do first. It's against the law to break into a police station. I could arrest you."

He'd like to see her try.

"I'm here for a… meeting," he said. Close enough to the truth. He had been hoping to see Julie. Just not in another man's arms.

Whatever it was she saw in his face must have reassured her because she lowered her weapon and returned it to its holster, though he noticed she left it unstrapped.

"Why don't you tell me who you're looking for and I'll see if they're around," she said, and ushered him toward the open doorway.

He hesitated. "Do you know who Julie Crenshaw was here to see?" he asked.

She frowned. "How do you know Ms. Crenshaw?"

Mike's brows lowered over the Ms. acronym. "She's a… relation."

"Well, maybe you should ask her then," came the tart reply. Then she relented and gave him his answer.

"She was here to see Detective O'Rourke. I'm afraid I can't say more than that." She must have seen his concern because she hurried to add, "Don't worry, she's not in trouble or anything."

He wished he could take her at her word, but something evil was lurking in his wife's shadow and Mike wasn't sure he could stop it.

The woman waited for him to leave the room before closing the door and joining him for the walk down the hall. He needed to get rid of her so he could vanish, but was loathe to do anything to scare her away. It had been too long since he'd had meaningful conversation with anyone other than Lucas. It felt... good.

He glanced sideways and admired the mink-like darkness of her hair in its prim and proper knot high on the back of her head. It only served to highlight the slim length of her neck and the shell of her ear. She was an attractive young woman. Why wasn't the detective making googly eyes at her instead of Jules?

"What's your name?" he abruptly asked, surprised that it mattered to him.

"Corporal Tate," she answered, sliding him a look from under thick brown lashes.

He smiled, aware she thought he was flirting with her—which he absolutely wasn't. "Your first name."

"It's Madison, Maddie to my friends." *Which we could be*, her tone seemed to say.

The little interchange helped to ease the choked emotion he'd had after seeing Jules. He was grateful to Corporal Tate, Maddie to her friends, for that, and for making him feel like an attractive man again, instead of a nonentity.

"I'm Michael," he told her. "Michael… Morning Star."

She gave him a doubtful look. "Well, Michael Morning Star, or whoever you are, next time try entering the way everyone else does and we won't have any misunderstandings."

If only that were possible.

"I'll try to remember that," Mike murmured, concern taking over now they were nearing the front of the department. He wasn't visible to anyone else, or at least he hadn't been. How was he going to explain that to the woman by his side? *Sorry, ma'am, I forgot to mention you've been chit-chatting with a freaking ghost.*

He grasped her arm, anxious to delay the moment when his reality kicked in and he'd have to return to his lonely non-existence.

She let out a soft gasp, and stared up at him with wide whiskey-brown eyes. Mike met her gaze and was sucked into their mysterious depths.

His mind was filled with a vision of her in a stand of trees, her face white and frightened froze. He could sense her fear, feel the threat, but there was nothing he could do to stop what happened next. The figure of a man appeared, dressed head to toe in black, impossible to recognize. He crept toward Julie from behind, a gun pointed at her back.

Run, Julie. For God's sake, run.

The words were a silent scream reverberating up Mike's spine and exploding from his throat.

She turned, but it was too late. The man started toward her, his intent to kill stamped on his frame. The flash and resulting smack as she ducked, and threw herself sideways into a thick clump of shrubs and the bullet slammed into Maddie stopped his heart. The woods erupted into shouts as police swarmed the area.

Mike flew to the last place he'd seen Maddie, frantic to find her. But his relief at spotting her was short-lived. She lay prone, staring up into the star-filled sky, her gaze dazed, filled with shock and the knowledge of her impending death. He started to land, to do… something, but then the detective was there, leaning over her, begging her to stay with him.

And Maddie? Her eyes searched the sky so frantically he could almost hear her heart pounding, until she found him, hovering near the tree line. She relaxed, a tranquil expression placed a slight smile on her lips, and then she slid into a blessed sleep.

"What's wrong?"

Her voice jarred him back to the present. He stared down at the pretty young police officer and had to bite back the warnings hovering on the tip of his tongue. She'd never believe him anyway. He vowed right then to watch over her and ensure she was given the chance to enjoy a long, happy life, as he had not.

He smiled into her upturned face. "I just wanted to thank you for your kindness. Have a good life, Maddie Tate."

She tipped her head and looked at him like he had a screw loose. She was probably right.

Just then another officer called from down the hall. "Hey, Madison. Do you know what happened to the McGregor folder?"

She sighed and opened the door marked archives. "I told you I was going to file it, Stan." She looked at Mike and shrugged. "Wait here, okay?"

She stepped into the room and flicked on the lights. Before she could return, he took the opportunity and vanished.

CHAPTER SEVENTEEN

Julie tried to focus on her interview with the mayor of Sooke and ignore the young officer standing near the whale watching tour sign. He probably thought he was being unobtrusive, but no one was fooled.

"Can you share what you are doing in the face of the perceived threat to your community?" Julie held the microphone steady and made sure Rudy had a clear shot of the mayor's reaction.

The mayor shared a reassuring smile with the camera, and a *don't-ask-me-questions-I-can't-answer*, glare with her. "Every measure is being taken to ensure the safety of our people, and of course, to track down the person behind this atrocity."

Julie waited for a stream of traffic to pass, grateful they weren't taping live. A fresh breeze off the ocean kept the heat from the spring sunshine at bay. It was one of those days where it seemed impossible that anything bad could happen—unfortunately for Cindy Blackthorn, the victim, it had. And other than reporting her name and that she had been a sex trade worker from Vancouver, the police were being very close-mouthed about the case. It bothered Julie that the woman was First Nations, and that there had been other cases of severed feet found along the coastline in the past few years. Some estimates placed the number of missing indigenous women and girls at over four thousand in Canada. Just how many were the work of serial killers?

A single bald eagle soared high above them in the cloudless blue sky.

Now that the camera was turned off the mayor asked the question obviously praying on everyone's mind. "Do you think the ABC Killer did this?"

Crap. She was going to choke whoever had come up with that awful tagline.

"It's too early to say, ma'am." Julie swiped the flat of her hand across her throat, signaling for Rudy to cut the film. She gazed sympathetically at the distraught woman. "He's probably long gone. He knows the police are looking for him, so he's not going to stick around. I wouldn't worry too much. However, you might want to do a press announcement warning people to take proper safety measures. Travel in pairs. Be aware of your surroundings. Lock your doors and windows."

The mayor nodded and rubbed shaky fingers over the creases lining her forehead. "I'll do that right away. This has always been a quiet town. I have two kids. I can't imagine how that poor woman's family feels right now. It's so frightening."

Yes, it was.

Detective O'Rourke—she had to think of him that way instead of the man who had kissed her and turned her world inside out—hadn't shared many details, but Ron had good sources in the coroner's office and they swore the victim had been raped and brutalized until death.

She touched the mayor's hand. "The RCMP are following up on some good leads. They'll get whoever did this. Don't worry, okay?"

The older woman nodded and squared her shoulders. "Are we done here? I'd like to go home and be with my family."

Julie knew that feeling. "Of course. Thank you for your time."

She waited for the mayor to get into her car and drive away before following Rudy to the news van.

Sam gazed sympathetically from inside the open back doors where they had already begun the job of splicing together the segments for tonight's broadcast. "Tough one."

Julie nodded. "I don't envy her position. She has to show a brave face for the town, when inside the fear of how close that creep was must be tearing her apart."

Sam glanced at Rudy rolling cable. The two of them had been married long enough that they shared each other's thoughts. It made Julie both envious and sad. She and Mike had been married eight years before the accident, but it had been so full of working and raising kids that they hadn't had a lot of time alone. Something she regretted now.

Her friend jumped out of the van, her hiking boots paired with cargo shorts, raising a little cloud of dust in the gravel parking lot. Construction on a new housing complex carried on behind them, a stark contrast to the blue of the Juan de Fuca Strait and the deep coastal forest across the bay. They'd chosen the location carefully, with the goal of showing the economic growth of the town. It was bad enough they had to report a murder here, they didn't want to have a negative impact on the town's tourism industry.

"Listen, you and the boys should come stay with us for a while." Sam sent a pointed look at the patrolman heading toward his unmarked police car. "It would be fun."

Julie smiled, warmed by the kindness of the offer. "Thanks, but you wouldn't say that if you saw Dustin and Freddy's bedrooms." She leaned over and gave Sam a quick hug. "I thank my stars that I have you guys on my team."

Sam's eyes were a little damp, but she shrugged it off with a grin, ever the tough girl. "Hey, we're just tagging along waiting for you to get the Pulitzer."

Julie laughed. "You're good for the ego, my friend. Don't worry, *when* we win, you'll be right up there with me. Even if it is in hiking boots." They glanced down at Sam's well-worn footwear.

Rudy chimed in from the back of the van, "It would have to be, she'd wear those damn things to bed if she could."

Sam only smiled, well used to her hubby's sarcasm. "You told me you thought it was sexy when I came to bed in my boots."

A deep red flush climbed the sides of his neck, though his eyes filled with a warm glow. "Oh, it was, darlin', it was."

Julie turned away, ostensibly to give the lovebirds some space, but in reality it caused an ache inside she wasn't sure how to handle. Visions of Connor filled her mind. His powerful body holding her close. The deepening intent from his mercurial gray eyes. His full lips.

Now she was the one getting hot.

She was fantasizing about a man. It was both new and strange. And edged in guilt.

"We'll see you back at the station," Sam called, slamming the van doors.

Julie waved over her shoulder and headed to her car, sitting all by its lonesome under the shade of a giant maple tree. Half an hour back to town if the traffic wasn't too bad, a couple of hours' work getting the story together, and she could go home and relax. Her mom and dad had been urging her to send the boys for a visit. She'd hesitated to pull them out of school so close to the end of the year, but with spring break starting next week maybe it would be a good time for them to go. Besides, she'd used the boys as a crutch for long enough. It wouldn't hurt her to be alone for a couple of weeks.

Before she could change her mind, Julie dug her cell phone out of her purse and speed-dialed her parents.

"Julie, we were just speaking about you," her mom's familiar voice made Julie's throat clench with emotion.

"Hi, Mom. Are you telling tales, again?" Her mother was famous for sharing embarrassing stories about Julie's childhood to her friends.

"Of course not, darling. What do you take me for?" The muted masculine tones in the background told Julie her dad was home from his job as a building inspector. "Oh, John, I do not."

Julie grinned. These three-way conversations were as much a part of home as the Friday night meatloaf her mom always made, and Julie and her father always complained about.

"Listen, I was wondering if your offer to take the kids was still standing?"

Her mom squealed in delight, deafening Julie's eardrum. "John, the boys are coming for a visit. Oh, my lord, there's so much to do. I need to clean their rooms and do some baking. Maybe we can take them to the Space Science Centre and the museum. Oh, and the movies. We have to take them to the movies." Her voice grew faint as she no doubt searched for her pad of paper and a pen. She kept notes for everything. It used to drive Julie crazy, but now that she was getting older, she saw the wisdom in her mother's old-fashioned ways.

Her dad came on the line and Julie's heart swelled. "Hello, my girl. Are you coming home too? We miss you."

"Hi, Daddy. I miss you too, but I have a job now. I'll book holidays and come see you later this summer, sound good?" It would be nice to go home. While they were settling into island life, Julie still missed Chicago and all her friends.

"You bet, sugar. We'll look forward to it. Here's your mother. I'll let you girls make the arrangements. We can't wait to see the boys, I bet they're growing like weeds."

Julie smiled through her tears. "They sure are. Dustin is almost as tall as I am now, and Freddy is coming up fast. They'll be so excited, they love staying at Grandma and Papa's house."

"And we love having them," he answered, his voice a little choked. "Take care of yourself, honey. You'll always be our little girl."

A few more words with her mom and Julie ended the connection, heart sore, but happy too. Whenever she felt down, all she had to do was think of her parents and she wasn't lonely anymore.

Relieved that she'd made the call, Julie started the car and pulled up to the highway, waiting for the traffic to slow so she could head for town. She couldn't wait to share the news with her sons. They were going to be over the moon. Grandma and Papa always spoiled them rotten. She was a little worried because it would be their first plane ride on their own, but her dad had assured her there were attendants to watch over them during the flight, and he'd be at the gate when they landed. She had to give them room to grow, she knew that. But nothing in the parent handbook said she had to like it.

The traffic was thinning so Julie flicked on her signal light, slid her sunglasses onto the end of her nose to guard against the punishing rays of the sun, and eased onto the pavement. She didn't white-knuckle it as much as she had just after the accident, but there were still times when her nerves threatened to get the better of her.

The muted roar of a diesel engine shifting gears had her glancing quickly into her rearview mirror. A semi was pulling onto the merge lane from the construction site, black smoke bellowing out of its chrome stacks like angry exclamation marks. She shivered, and was relieved when the police cruiser and a pickup passed him by to fall into line behind her. Now that she'd had a few days to get over her mad-on, Julie was secretly glad she had a bodyguard. The more she learned about the so-called ABC Killer, the more she prayed he was caught soon.

CHAPTER EIGHTEEN

The dumb bitch. She was stirring up fear with her stupid news reports. He had to be careful. No mistakes. He was tempted to follow her home and teach her a lesson about spreading lies. His momma had ground that rule into him in a way he'd never forget.

He lifted his leg too fast and dropped the clutch, swearing when the cab bucked. The rear lights stayed off on the cruiser in front of him. He sighed his relief and rubbed away the ghost pains before trying to shift again—properly this time.

He hadn't noticed the cop escort until it was almost too late, he'd been so focused on his quarry. It could have been a fatal error. He needed to get off the island for a while. Let things cool down.

The hunger hummed, an itch he could scratch but never eradicate. His momma had started it, the night she brought those men home. They'd hurt him. He'd cried for Momma to make it stop, too small to end it himself, but she'd just laid there on the sofa, her clothes half off and a white smear on her nose. They'd taken turns, those men, and all he could do was focus on his momma's tattooed breast, bared for all to see, and plan his revenge.

It took a few years, but he'd made it his business to find them, and he did. After meting out justice, he returned home and presented his momma proof of his vengeance—two severed left feet.

She hadn't understood.

"What did you do?" she cried, her once pretty face twisted with disgust.

He smiled, still riding high on his success. "I did what you taught me. Someone does something wrong, they gots to pay." He sat at the beat up old dining room table in their stuffy mobile home and stared at the half-finished puzzle spread across the surface. "I thought you'd be proud of me."

"Stupid child." She clouted his head hard enough to make it spin. "You can't hurt someone just because you feel like it."

A roar filled his ears. When it cleared he'd thrown her on the table, his hands around her throat. Her eyes were wide, pleading to be released. Garish red lips, the top one edged in a river of lines betraying years of hard living, panted for air he didn't feel like giving her. The power was heady. His head swam with it. His fingers tightened, the skin bulging as he pinched her throat closed like a vise. Veins lifted and turned blue on her cheeks and forehead, fighting for the oxygen they'd been deprived of, and still he pressed. He squeezed until the Holy Ghost escaped. Her eyes turned milky and mouth went lax. Then he sat down and added another piece to the puzzle.

A horn blared, and he blinked, the police cruiser in front of him coming back into focus. He eased up on the gas pedal, adding space between their vehicles. He gazed regretfully as the white Civic sped away.

Another time. I'll be back, bitch.

***

Connor opened the door of the tattoo parlor, his gaze cataloging the dismal interior as he searched for Matt's source. He found him perched on a stool bent over the shapely back of a young woman receiving a cherry blossom on her lower hip.

"Marko?"

Other than a slight tensing of the shoulders, the man showed no reaction. "Who wants to know?"

"Detective Connor O'Rourke with the RCMP. We need to talk." Connor rested his hand on the butt of his gun and waited.

The young woman jumped, causing Marko to flinch. "Hold still," he snapped. He sighed and sat back, lifting the magnifying glasses he'd been wearing to the top of his gray head. "I've got nothing to say." He nudged the girl to get up.

She scrambled to leave, towel slipping low on the back and riding high on the thighs.

"Tough job," Connor said, attempting some levity to gain the man's confidence.

"What do you want, man? I already told the cops everything I know." He shoved the stool back, the rollers squeaking their annoyance, and strode over to a coffee maker with a pot of black sludge resting on the burner. He poured himself a shot, went to replace the carafe and must have second-guessed his rudeness to an officer because he held it up for Connor.

Con took one look at the murky goo and shook his head. "No time, thanks. This isn't about the other day. We have your report. I need to know what you were going to tell my partner, Matthew Roy."

Marko glared, motioning with his chin to the curtain hanging over the change room door. Connor nodded and suppressed his impatience until the woman stepped out in a sleek slip dress in iridescent green.

"Same time next week?" she asked, her attention on Connor.

"Yeah, I'll get it finished then," Marko said, his gaze mocking her obvious attempt at flirtation.

They waited until she reluctantly left, then Marko locked the door and pulled the shades. He met Connor's eyes and shrugged. "I don't want no trouble."

Considering the length of the guy's rap sheet, that ship had sailed, but Connor refrained from commenting. "Matt said you had some info about a tattoo we found on a murder victim?"

Marko rubbed his jaw, then opened a panel previously hidden behind an inked sketch of Betty Boop riding a Harley, a saucy grin on her cherry red lips. He removed a drawing from the vault and handed it over. "This it?"

A rush of excitement heated Connor's veins. The sketch was a near perfect illustration of the brand. The only difference was a serpent slithering through the middle of a rectangular puzzle piece instead of the elongated *S*.

"Where did you get this?" he demanded.

Marko took a step back, his hands up in the classic stop motion. "Relax, man. I made it, okay? A client ordered it done, but then backed out, said he was scared of needles or some shit. He insisted on buying the print though, paid real good for it too."

Connor flicked the corner of the paper. "What's this then?"

Marko grinned, a sly look entering his wily green eyes. "Job security, man. Job security."

CHAPTER NINETEEN

Lucas sat in the Chicago park where he'd first come to the gut-wrenching realization that life as he'd known it was over. No more Hollywood. No more chances to see his name on blockbuster movie posters leading the pack of hungry wolves that made up the acting industry. No more thrill of success.

He stared out across the verdant green grass to a pond in the distance, absently noting the baby ducks following their momma to the water's edge. The last time he'd been here, autumn had cut a swathe through the park, leaving dead and decaying leaves in its wake.

The period in between had passed in the blink of an eye, and at the same time, depressingly slow.

Two young boys erupted onto the field, pushing and shoving and giggling as only young kids do. They had a soccer ball and spread out to pass it back and forth. They weren't bad too for their ages, the ball skimming the ground effortlessly with dexterous kicks like a well-choreographed play. Suddenly the ball took off as though possessed, heading straight for the unsuspecting ducklings waddling docilely behind their mother.

Lucas jumped to his feet, heart racing with the certain knowledge of impending death. He sent a silent, urgent message to the nearest child, but it was too late. There was no way to stop what was about to happen. His human body was too big, too slow, he'd never reach them in time.

The momma duck must have picked up on the danger. She whirled around, assessed the threat, and barked an order that sent her babies scurrying into the water. Instead of following where she would have had hope of safety, she stood her ground, head high, hissing and snapping, determined to guard her young to the death. Stupid bird. She couldn't beat a hard rubber ball. She'd be injured, possibly fatally. What would her babies do then?

Desperate to end the unnecessary heroism of the bird, Lucas bounded across the lawn, arms flapping like a lunatic. The boys took one look at him and ran, crying, into the comforting arms of their mothers, who turned and hurried them away from the field.

He didn't give a shit. His only concern was with the family heading to a catastrophic ending—like Julie Crenshaw and her sons.

The duck's desperate bid to save her children became the woman in the van hurtling toward his car at what felt at the time like warp speed. He'd taken lives that day, including his own. Lucas couldn't stand by and see it happen again.

A familiar pain ripped through his shoulder blades, causing him to stumble. He regained his footing in time to take air, the wings he'd been gifted with upon his entry to Heaven's door opening with a snap like a sail catching the breeze. He arrowed across the remaining distance, and with a fist resembling a mallet, sent the ball spiraling into the tree tops far across the field.

The duck squawked, apparently not impressed with his celestial beauty, and waddled away to join her young. Lucas stared, nonplussed. Then the absurdity hit him and he chuckled. Once started he couldn't seem to stop and tears rolled down his cheeks. Dead, and the best he could do was catch shit from a bird.

"Hey, buddy. Long time no see."

The voice of his childhood friend startled him. Lucas swung around and brushed the signs of his weakness away. Scott Anderson stood in a patch of sunlight, his blond hair and white smile so bright it hurt the eyes.

Lucas swayed, overcome by a mixture of sorrow and love for this man who was the brother he'd never had. He stepped into his buddy's arms and held tight, swallowing down the sappy words building in his throat.

Just shy of awkward, he leaned back, hands on Scott's shoulders to get a good look at his face. He seemed happy, relaxed. Oddly, his happiness bothered Lucas. "What are you doing here?"

Scott's brows drew together. "I come here all the time, bro. This was the only place I figured I might run into you. Looks like I was right. Again." He winked and feinted with a light punch that bounced off Lucas' stomach.

Lucas calmed. He should be glad his friend was doing well. Moving on.

Life was for living, that was their slogan.

It wasn't Scott's fault Lucas was spinning his wheels with no idea where he was going. What he should be doing. He'd lived his entire life with the single-minded goal to succeed. Now, when he should be at peace, he was floundering.

"How have you been?" He hesitated. "I've… missed you."

Scott gave him a one armed man-hug and they started across the grass toward the gazebo. Lucas grinned, remembering the stunned look on his friend's face when he'd materialized as an angel and scared the shit out of some teens who'd set their sights on the mourning movie star.

"Remember those kids?" he said, pointing toward the shelter, glowing a soft white in the afternoon light.

Scott laughed. "Boy, do I. They practically left skid marks getting away that night."

They strode on in silence, the awkwardness returning.

What was the matter with him? He should be walking on air right now. His buddy was here. And better yet, he could actually see him and talk to him. Lucas wasn't alone any more.

"Are you still seeing the ME?" he asked, determined to overcome this... this jealousy burning a hole in his gut.

"Yeah, I am," Scott answered, his gaze going all moony-eyed. "I think she's the one, buddy. I'm going to ask her to marry me." He stopped and grabbed Lucas' arm. "I wished you were here. I've been praying for you to come. I want you to be my best man."

He swallowed hard and swore under his breath. He didn't deserve this man for a friend. Here he'd been, feeling sorry for himself while Scott had been dreaming the impossible.

"Fuck, man, you know I would," he ground out, teeth clenched around the pain.

Scott gave him a mega-watt smile, the one that had made him into a superstar. "It's not over, 'til it's over. You taught me that."

Lucas decided not to remind him that he'd also taught him not to reach for the stars, they had a tendency to fall.

"So what's it like, being Master of the Universe?" Scott teased. "You've got some serious props there." He nodded to the wings folded on Lucas' back. "They've changed color, haven't they?"

Lucas glanced over his shoulder and took in the downy gray feathers. Hmm, it seemed like the shade varied depending on his actions. Do something out of anger, they turned a dark thunderous gray. Do something out of compassion, they lightened. Could that be the key? He was almost certain Mike was holding Natalya beyond the gates, but since he'd been denied access so far…

He shrugged. "Maybe a couple of shades. I don't know, I don't get to use them often."

Climbing the stairs was like stepping back in time. The same wicker furniture he'd found Scott passed out on after the accident occupied a corner of the room, though now it was arranged to take advantage of the sun streaming in from the east. A broom for cleaning—maybe the same one Scott used to fend off their attackers?—rested against the wall near a rustic picnic table and a potbelly wood stove, both new additions.

Change. Everything was changing. He needed to learn to accept that and move on with what the Lord had in store for him. Or be left in that no-where-land between Heaven and earth forever.

"Any word on Nat?" Scott asked, as though reading his mind.

He wished he had better news. "Not yet. I'll find her though. I can't tell you how…"

Scott raised his hand, stopping the flow of words. "Let it go, man. It's eating you up inside. There was nothing you could do. Don't take this wrong, 'cause you gotta know I'd do anything to have you guys back, but I'm happy now. If it hadn't happened I might never have met Tracy and fallen in love." He sat on top the picnic table, long legs dangling off the side like a school kid. "She's amazing, bro. I wish you two could meet."

They could, he'd just be a middle-aged cabbie when it happened.

"Sure, one big family reunion, right?" He didn't make any attempt to hide his bitterness. How could Scott act as if nothing had happened?

A family entered the gazebo, an overflowing picnic basket dangling from the father's grip. The young mother caught sight of Scott spotlighted by a shaft of sunlight as though blessed by the Gods and her eyes went wide, her grip tight on her boys' hands.

"Honey," she whisper-shrieked. "Honey, that's Scott Anderson."

Scott grimaced, before turning a charming smile onto the family. His worried gaze met Lucas' over the heads of the children as they swarmed him, making it obvious he'd picked up on his friend's discontent.

Lucas was surprised at the lack of envy he felt. In the early days he and Scott had made a game out of counting their fans. They'd both craved the notoriety, and the escape from their early dirt-poor lives. Once they'd achieved their fame though, it hadn't taken long to pall. There was virtually no privacy, and everyone wanted to use them for their money— including their agent who'd gone so far as to commit murder in order to cover his embezzlement of their funds. And had almost killed Scott in the process.

He stood back, once again invisible, and watched his buddy win the family over with charm and easy laughter, no doubt turning them into fans for life.

Yeah, he was one lucky bastard all right.

CHAPTER TWENTY

Julie had been sitting at her desk for the past two hours and hadn't achieved much in the way of words for tonight's story. What she had found was a disturbing trail of bodies and very little to link them together.

She sat back and stared at the computer screen, chewing the end of her pencil. Did the police realize how widespread these cases were? They had to. If this was the work of one killer, he'd been doing it for at least ten years or more. The first victim was found in a farmer's field in Flin Flon, Manitoba, and like this case, she'd been discovered with a jagged stump where her left foot should have been. Then, there was the teenager found in a gravel pit in New Brunswick. Her only similarity to the present case came from the viciousness of the assault and the strangulation as cause of death.

She took a sip from her cup and grimaced. Yuck, cold coffee just wasn't the same.

He was escalating, learning his MO. The more he killed, the more choreographed it became. He knew his moves. Knew what he had to do in order to capture them without getting noticed. And how to extend his torture until he was ready to let them die.

She shivered and turned to grab the cardigan hanging on the back of her chair.

And shrieked.

Ron had his nose practically buried in her ear.

"What the hell, Henderson? Personal space a new concept for you?" She wiped ineffectively at the splotches on her dark slacks. Thanks to him giving her a heart attack she'd spilled her coffee.

He straightened, his gaze turning from amused to quizzical as he fixated on the reports she'd pulled up on the computer. "Whatcha got going there?" He nodded to the screen.

Julie hurried to one-click the program closed. "Nothing that concerns you."

Ron smirked. "Is that any way to treat your fellow co-worker, Miss Crenshaw?"

He reached over, picked up her coffee mug, and helped himself to a drink. Julie hid her smile, impressed that he kept a straight face, though he was quick to set the cup down.

"Serves you right. Next time get your own," she said.

"You're such a hardass, Crenshaw." He hooked a leg around a nearby chair and pulled it up to the desk. "C'mon, we're supposed to be a team. Your news is my news, and my news is... my news." He grinned.

Julie shook her head. "I'm not surprised you don't have a girlfriend, Ron. You're an egotistical jerk."

He shrugged. "Guilty as charged. Now tell me what you were looking at with such intensity."

The urge to keep all her findings under wraps so she could be the one to break the story and finally prove her value, vied with the guilt she'd feel if anyone else got hurt while she was attempting to climb the corporate ladder.

Common sense won.

She clicked the computer back to life and turned the screen so he could see it better. "You remember that foot I found at the beach a couple of weeks ago?"

He nodded, his gaze for once sympathetic. "Yeah, that had to be pretty nasty."

She repressed a shudder. "It was." Her pencil tapped the screen where she'd been struggling with her report. "I went to Sooke today. They found a body. Maybe *my* body."

Ron glanced over, his bottle-green eyes soft. "I'm sorry, kiddo. No one should ever die that way."

Julie swallowed hard. It was damn near impossible not to imagine the depravities this woman and all the others she'd been investigating had gone through. It made her angry and helpless and incredibly sad that anyone could do something like this to another human being.

"I did some backdoor searches." She met his gaze. "Don't ask. Anyway, I've pieced together a trail of murders dating back almost ten years that have never been solved and have one or more similarities to our guy. Take a look at these old newspaper clippings." She clicked one after the other, more than twenty in total.

Ron frowned and leaned forward to read. "This could be random, Julie. There's no way to prove it's linked to our case." He paused. "Even if our competitors want to jump the gun and yell serial killer."

She clenched her hands and gritted her teeth. "You think I don't know how dangerous this is? We could cause mass hysteria and have the whole country in an uproar." Too upset to sit any longer, she shoved away from the desk and stood, the casters squawking on the cement flooring. "But if I'm right and we do nothing to stop this guy, are you going to be able to sleep with yourself?"

"That's the only way I get any rest," Ron said, ever the mouthpiece. But his attention was on her files. She was on to something. She could feel it.

"Have you talked to your cop boyfriend about any of this?"

His glance made her uncomfortable. She swiped her cup out from beside his elbow before he bumped it to the floor, and strode to the single cup brewer she'd treated herself to when she got the job offer.

"He's not my boyfriend, and no, I haven't. Yet."

Ron stood and moved to her side, towering at least six inches over her head. If he were into intimidation his linebacker body, tattooed arms, and enigmatic eyes would deter most people, but she knew he wasn't like that. For all his cynicism, Ron was a good guy.

"You can't, Jules."

She stiffened. Her nickname on another man's lips instead of Mike's still had the power to bring her to her knees.

"This story could be our big break," he carried on, unaware he'd just set off a bomb in her heart. "Look, I'm not saying we *don't* tell your... friend. I'm just saying we could pick the time."

He wanted her to sit on what could be the story of a lifetime. But if she did, and someone else died...

What was she going to do?

CHAPTER TWENTY-ONE

Mike landed a few feet from the cave he'd found not long after the accident that had taken his life. Funny really, when he'd opened his eyes that day he'd assumed they were at the park having a picnic and he'd fallen asleep.

Now, same as then, the sky was an impossible robin's egg blue, so bright he had to squint to see across the waving green grass of an endless meadow. But unlike that day, his children were not playing tag, and his beautiful, pregnant wife wasn't lying at his side.

He was alone.

Tired, he made his way to the mouth of the cave and entered. The light faded the further he walked, not that it mattered, his eyes were sharp as an owl's in the dark. Just one of the many changes his body had undergone in its transition to the other side. On earth he'd fallen from a tree as a child and broken his leg in two places. It had left him with a slight limp and a cool scar to show his friends. That was gone now. He'd been gifted with the taller, stronger, healthier version in this world, but he'd take his beaten up body any day if it gave him his life back.

As with most things in Heaven, the cave wasn't your typical damp, cold, dirt and bats affair. This cave was the Taj Mahal of caves. Its walls were thick slabs of smooth granite, onyx black with striations of gold weaving throughout like a road map. The first time he'd entered, he'd been astounded to come across the emerald green pool off one of the passageways. A three-foot waterfall tumbled over what looked like a small landslide and fed the pool from the far end of the room. The water had beckoned. He'd stripped down and dove in, gasping at the cleansing coolness. And that's where he'd discovered the secret room, hidden behind the waterfall.

It became his sanctuary.

Then the Lord, in all his wisdom, paired Mike with the very person who had caused his death and revenge led him to kidnap a young woman who had no idea what she'd done wrong. An innocent. And now, all he wanted was to set her free and maybe thereby gain a little peace. It had taken him far too long, but he could finally see that it had been an accident. No one was at fault, or if there was a guilty person, he was in jail. Mike had learned Lucas was drugged the day of the crash, his agent's desperate bid to cover a trail full of lies and deceit.

Greed. Was there ever a more hateful word?

Mike dove beneath the falls and came up on the other side. He climbed onto the narrow ledge rimming what looked like a solid wall except for an oddly colored rock sticking about a quarter of an inch above the smooth surface near the edge of the water. He placed his hand palm down on the rock and pressed. There was a momentary lull, and then with a shudder that shook his body, the wall slid to the right, disappearing into the face of the hill like a pocket door.

Natalya was sitting cross-legged on the bed, her feet tucked up under her thighs, reading one of the romance novels he'd found at the Transition House and brought for her entertainment. She jumped like a startled doe and leaped to her feet, the book tumbling to the floor.

"Easy," Mike said, concerned she would hurt herself. "How are you, little one?"

She put a hand to her breast as though to still its rapid-fire beat, then bent and carefully picked up the hard-bound book and returned it to the shelf along one wall. When she turned back to him her features were wary.

"What do you want?" Her gaze slid to the door he'd deliberately left open, before coming back to challenge him. "Unless you're letting me go, I don't need you here." Her body language said *get lost* with stiff shoulders and clenched fists, but her eyes were vulnerable, and so lonely it ripped his guts out. He should have released her long ago. Hell, he never should have taken her to begin with.

"That's what I wanted to speak to you about." He gestured toward the table and chairs. "Can we talk?"

She shrugged, but walked across the thick carpet to take a seat. Mike frowned. Her feet were bare, he hadn't brought her any shoes. She must have gotten chilled, but hadn't once complained. He was an ass.

He cleared his throat and took the other chair. "Have you been well since I was last here?" he asked, his tongue tripping awkwardly over the words.

Natalya glared. "What do you care? That's the whole idea of kidnapping me, isn't it? To make me suffer?"

He winced. Okay, she was bitter. Mike could understand that. He'd make it up to her somehow, if she'd let him.

"It was never about you, honey. This was between me and Lucas. I'm sorry I placed you in the middle when you've already been through enough."

She eyed him like he was pond scum. "Just say it. You mean because I'm dead. We're *all dead*." Her voice climbed an octave. "I'm sick and tired of tiptoeing around the reality. You need to figure out how you're going to deal, because there is no going back."

For all that she looked like an angel with long white-blond hair and sky blue eyes, she didn't pull any punches. Not that he didn't deserve a tongue-lashing. Stealing her away from the Transition House and locking her in this cave—even if it was homey—had been the wrong thing to do. Too bad hindsight was always twenty-twenty.

"I realize that now," he said. "I've come to return you to Lucas."

He hadn't expected her to jump for joy and give him a hug—though it would have been nice—but he certainly never thought she'd throw her hands up into the air and cry "Men!" either. He sat back and stared at her, bemused. "What?"

She stood and paced the room, mumbling words he couldn't hear, and a few he wished he hadn't.

"Your mama teach you to talk that way?" If his daughter ever swore like... the pang was more the ache of an old wound now, rather than that of a fresh slice. She would have been beautiful—like her mother—and cherished.

He sat up, a sudden thought occurring to him. If he had landed up here with Lucas and Natalya, was it possible his daughter was nearby? Maybe there was a level for innocent children, ones who had never done wrong. How could he find out? The Lord could tell him. He needed to go back to…

Something smashed against the back of his head. He grunted and started to lift a hand to the pain when it struck again. Dazed, he stood, only to lose his balance and topple to the floor.

Darkness closed in. An angel bent over his prone body, tears swimming in brilliant blue eyes. Then, there was nothing.

CHAPTER TWENTY-TWO

Julie stumbled past the crowds tugging suitcases and cranky children into the international airport. She stopped near the totems towering against a brilliant blue sky, sank onto a bench, and stared blankly at the parking lot. Her babies were gone. It was for the best, and they were thrilled to be traveling on an airplane—alone—to visit their grandparents, but... her babies were gone. They'd never been apart, not even after Mike and baby Ava died.

The ache was an echo of that earlier pain, the one that had ripped her heart from her chest. Even though they were only away for a short while, it already seemed like forever. Mike had loved the boys and always made time for them, even after a long day at work. She was trying, but being a single parent was hard. The responsibility for their care sometimes seemed overwhelming, but there was no choice, they relied on her.

She wiped her eyes and rose, determined to shake off her morose mood. The kids were safe, that was the important thing. As soon as Connor caught the suspect they could come home, until then she had a job to do.

Her car was parked at the end of a seemingly endless row of fancy imports and luxury models. The old Civic stood out like a sore thumb. So did the tall, grim man leaning his mouth-watering butt against the front fender.

Her heart stuttered. She hesitated, then strode forward. "What are you doing here?"

He straightened and met her halfway. "I heard what you were doing and thought you might like a little support," he said, his gray eyes soft.

She looked down, unwilling to show her vulnerability. "I'm fine. They'll probably get spoiled silly at my mom's." Then the rest of what he said sank in. She glared. "What does that mean, 'You heard what I was doing?' There's no way even your lackey could have known why I was at the airport," she said.

Shocked, she patted her body down and searched through her purse. "Did you bug me, Detective?"

Connor grabbed her hands, stilling her frantic movements. He lifted her chin so she had to meet his gaze. "Calm down, okay?" He waited until she gave an aggravated nod. "No, I did not have a listening device planted on your person. My *lackey*, as you call him, informed me that you were on the way to the airport. It was a simple matter to call the service counter and check the flights." He squeezed her hand then released it. "I thought you might be leaving town." He stared at her. "I had to know."

What was he saying? Why would it matter to him if she went away for a while? He should be happy to have her gone, she was using up valuable resources with her police guard. Unless…

"You don't need to worry," she said, lifting her chin. "Even if I had left town, I would have been back when your case went to trial. I fully realize I'm a possible key witness."

Disappointment lay like a heavy weight over her chest. She should have known. He wasn't there for her, he was only trying to protect his investment. Make sure all the I's were dotted when he finally caught the person behind these murders. She squared her shoulders. *Quit feeling sorry for yourself.* That's where her focus should be also, getting justice for the families suffering the loss of their loved ones. Not worrying whether some man might miss her if she was gone, or not.

"Julie." He reached out, but then let his hand drop.

She hated to admit she ached for his touch.

He gestured toward her car. "Let me drive you home."

She stared at him, perplexed. "Why?"

He shrugged and attempted a lame joke. "I always wanted to see what went into fifty years of racing technology."

Instead of the intended laughter, his words made the hair squirm on the back of her neck. "What's going on, Connor? Why are you really here?"

He glanced around the lot, then ushered her into the car on the passenger side. "I'll tell you once we get out of here."

He was making her feel like there was a giant target pinned to her back, which was silly. Why would the killer come after her? She knew little about the case, and finding that foot on the beach, while horrifying, was certainly not enough to lead the police to whoever was behind the crime. Unless they did find something…?

He closed her door and strolled around the front of the car, and her heart fluttered. The wind caressed his tobacco brown locks, sending a few hairs tumbling across his forehead. He impatiently brushed them aside, his forearm bunching with muscle. When he climbed in, his shoulders took up much of the space in the front seat. When had her car become so small?

He spent a few moments rearranging her driver's seat and setting the mirrors, then did up his seatbelt, his hand coming way too close to her hip for comfort. Then he quit moving around and looked at her with a raised brow.

It took her a second to get with the program and dig around in her bag for the keys, her cheeks uncomfortably hot. She dropped them into his open hand and waited, anxious to open her window and get some air that didn't smell of pine and testosterone.

Connor started the car and chuckled when the engine gave its customary burp, burp, groan, before turning over. "This is some hotrod you have." He grinned and her stomach did cartwheels. "Do up your seatbelt."

She grimaced, but did as he asked. It took a few miles of white-knuckling the seat under her thighs before Julie could settle down and acknowledge his expertise behind the wheel during the heavy highway traffic, but she still hugged the door to give him plenty of room for maneuvering.

He glanced over and smiled. "Relax, Julie, I'm not going to wreck your baby here."

She clenched her fingers around the seatbelt hugging her chest and tried to do as he suggested. The ocean peek-a-booed behind stands of arbutus and maple trees. It was impossible to retain her

melancholy mood with views like that. And the
detective wasn't bad either.

"So you going to tell me why you wasted half your
morning to chase after me?" she asked.

He signaled and passed a tractor trudging down the
road, waited until it was safe, then slid smoothly back
into the right lane before he answered. "Our guy is
escalating." His fingers tightened on the steering
wheel. "Another severed foot was found this
morning, honey." He reached over and clasped her
hand and she realized she'd started to tremble.

Where?"

"Vancouver, along the Sunshine Coast highway."

She could feel his concerned gaze, but kept her
head turned away, barely noticing the fields and
homes that flashed by interspersed with an obscene
stretch of billboards advertising everything from
whale tours to moving companies.

Another foot.

Another young woman who would never grow old
enough to hold her grandchildren. As a parent, Julie

ached for the girl's family. As a woman, she mourned the loss of her virtue. Her life.

Why was he doing this? What made him hate women so much that he had to violate not only their bodies, but their very souls?

"We're going to get him." Connor said, but she wasn't so sure. And that's when she knew she had to tell him everything she and Ron had found.

She turned to face him and took a moment to study the hard angles of his nose and jaw. This was a man's man. She could easily picture him kicking back with the boys, teaching them how to shoot hoops, or cast a fishing rod. He had a love of the outdoors written all over him, from his reddish brown tan to the deep lines by the corners of his eyes caused by squinting into the sun.

She liked him, and she respected his judgement. So whether Ron wanted to go for the big story or not, she needed to come clean.

"You have a few minutes when we get there?" she asked, and blushed when he gave her a look laden with male interest. "I... I have something I want to show you." Okay, that came out wrong. "About the case. It might help."

The smile died out of his eyes, and left them a steely gray. "Sure, I need to wait for a ride to my car anyway."

She'd be ruining her chance with the station. They wouldn't want to keep her after this. They'd have to move back to Chicago, but it didn't matter. As long as they caught the killer, she'd be happy.

Even if it meant leaving Connor behind.

CHAPTER TWENTY-THREE

Connor kept his eyes on the busy highway, though he was hyper-aware of the woman sitting inches away. The open windows let in the fresh spring breeze along with the roar of traffic. It also played havoc with Julie's golden-brown hair. Every time the honeyed strands caressed the skin of his forearm he quivered, the sensation as erotic as her kisses.

He had to concentrate to keep his foot light on the gas pedal when all the while his little head urged him to race home, drag her into the house, and not come out for a week. Of course that wasn't going to happen. She'd probably deck him if he tried, but that didn't stop the fantasy from playing out in his mind.

She'd dressed for her day off in a pair of mint green mid-thigh shorts and a white t-shirt with the logo, *Moms know best*. His momma never looked like that. Those shorts were driving him crazy. Whenever she moved, the material inched higher, tempting him to help. Her skin, touched with a slight blush from the early summer sun, looked like the finest velvet, soft and smooth and oh-so lush.

He shifted and hoped like hell she wouldn't notice what she did to him. He reached over and switched on the radio, surprised when hip hop blared out of the tinny speakers. He met her gaze with a raised eyebrow.

"What?" she asked. "I like upbeat music, okay?"

He grinned, charmed by her defensive attitude. "Sure. I just never pictured you as the street dancer type."

She looked at him and smiled, relaxing. God, he loved her smile. "I have moves," she said.

Oh, he didn't doubt that for a second. It was imagining her *moves* that was getting him into trouble.

"You'll have to show me some time," he murmured.

A comfortable silence fell between them. If it weren't for the fact a killer was on the loose and possibly after his girl here—His girl. Where did that come from? He slid her a sideways glance, and was treated to the vision of her lip-syncing and gyrating to the music, totally out of harmony and absolutely adorable.

It was like a sledgehammer nailed him square in the chest. He damn near hit the brakes.

He was falling for Julie Crenshaw.

His mouth went dry and he choked, coughing like a blinking idiot. Which he was. This was not good. Not good at all.

"Are you okay?" she asked, concern turning her eyes deep and mysterious as the rainforest. She patted his arm and he wanted to tell her he wasn't one of her kids, but the lump in his throat was growing from a tadpole into a bullfrog. He waved and nodded and blamed the moisture in his eyes on the dry cough.

"Swallowed wrong," he managed to get out and she nodded as though that made perfect sense.

"We're almost home. You can get a drink then."
She smiled with sympathy.

What he needed was a stiff shot of whiskey. He'd
sworn he would never go down this road again. The
last time he'd cared for a woman, she'd ended up
dead. Sex was fine. Good even. And there wasn't
room for regrets. But Julie wouldn't be that kind of a
relationship. She radiated home and hearth and
happily-ever-afters.

Not his kind of girl at all.

He turned into her driveway with a sense of relief.
At least now they could focus on the case and leave
all this other… personal goop behind.

The yard showed evidence of two active young
children. A basketball hoop was hung rather
drunkenly from the garage and waved in the breeze
above the hood of the car. A pedal bike lay on its side
on the edge of the sidewalk as though the owner had
just left it to run indoors, and a trampoline had been
set up near the corner of the house. A family lived
here. He'd known that before, of course. It just hadn't
really registered until now. Like a fool, in some far

off corner of his mind, he'd still been entertaining thoughts of getting her into bed.

Not anymore.

Julie had more than enough responsibilities on her plate. Even if a session of hotter-than-hell sex—and he had a feeling with her it would be scorching—was good for the soul, she'd suffer for it, and he wouldn't be able to live with himself if that happened.

So yeah, no sex.

Damn.

"Watch your step. I told the boys to clean up before they left, but you know how kids are." She grinned and opened the car door.

He followed behind, his skin not quite fitting right. She was an anomaly, Julie Crenshaw. She looked like a calendar pin-up girl, and yet was a crack reporter and a caring parent. Every time he turned around, she revealed another fascinating facet of her personality. Hell, she lip-synced for cripes sake.

How was he supposed to defend himself against that?

The house was dim after the brightness of the sun and felt like a cool sanctuary. One he didn't want to leave.

She set her bag down on the cluttered coffee table and headed down the hall toward the kitchen. "Coffee?"

Connor frowned, eyeing the assortment of coloring books and crayons. "Yeah, sure. Black's fine." He edged his way into the room and sat gingerly on the chesterfield with its faded plaid material. Probably safer than leather with kids. His sleek furniture would be as out of place as he was here. There were family photos on the wall behind him. Lots of the boys through their stages of growth, and one of Julie, beautiful as a princess in her wedding gown, her tall, lean husband gazing down into her face with adoration. They'd been a handsome couple and he fully expected to feel some jealousy, but instead it was empathy that flooded his chest. They'd had their whole lives in front of them, and in the blink of an eye it all changed.

It took him a long time after Karen died. They'd been living together in Vancouver for two years and he'd been working up to asking her to marry him when she'd been caught in the crossfire between two gangs. He'd never gotten the chance to say good-bye, she'd died on-scene, and he regretted it to this day.

"I want my kids to always remember what their father looked like." Julie entered the room, two steaming mugs of caffeinated goodness in her hands.

Connor stood and took one of the cups. "You're a good mother," he said, and meant it.

She laughed. "Not sure the boys would always agree with you." Her gaze went to her husband's picture and the infinite sadness hurt his heart. "He was a wonderful father."

She turned and set her cup with careful precision over a faded coffee ring left on the wood of the table and sat on the sofa instead of the room's only other chair.

Connor hesitated, not sure if he should move or resume his seat. He sighed, and sat. The weight of his body tipped the cushions and she rolled his way, stopping her momentum with a hand on his thigh.

He froze, not daring to so much as breathe.

Their eyes met.

Hers widened, no doubt because his was filled with a lust he couldn't control. She went to lift her hand and he stopped her, lacing their fingers together. Throwing common sense out the window, he carefully guided her palm in a slow glide up and down his leg, the muscles twitching beneath her touch.

Her mouth opened in a near-silent gasp and he gave in to the devil riding his shoulder and leaned over, intent on fulfilling his fantasy.

CHAPTER TWENTY-FOUR

The combination of rough denim and tensile muscle beneath her hand, and the molten steel of Connor's eyes, drew Julie into a web of sensual heat she was helpless to deny.

He leaned nearer and her heart beat wildly beneath her breast.

He was going to kiss her.

She forgot to breathe.

Finally, his lips met hers and the tension released with a soft sigh of acceptance. Her eyes slid closed, the better to take in all the sensations bombarding her senses. Mint and coffee. Musk and man. Good. So good. He took his time, teasing and tasting until she thought she'd go mad. His arm around her waist tugged her close. Hip to thigh, breast to chest. Mouth to mouth. Their bodies fit as though they were made for each other. He was all hard planes to her softer curves. Strong where she was weak. And yet, his hand trembled against the side of her face and his heart pounded beneath her fingertips.

The power was heady.

She affected this man. He wanted her. And she him. Julie couldn't deny the heat racing under her skin, or the swelling of her breasts. She ached for him. It was too much. It wasn't enough.

She opened her mouth and he swept in, conquering this new ground with a growl of approval that vibrated through her body and sent tingles between her thighs. His deft fingers unhooked her bra and followed the loosened material around to her nipples. The combination of his tongue mating with hers, and calloused fingers caressing her breast, created a maelstrom of want such as she'd never felt before.

No longer content to be the supplicant, Julie ran impatient fingers over the buttons of his chambray shirt, anxious to touch warm, hard muscle. To copy the path of turmoil he had caused. She left his mouth to spread kisses along his jaw, and reveled in his groan. Her lips moved lower, tugged at an earlobe, nipped at the pulse jumping in his neck. Down, down, past the opening she'd made in his shirt. Over a taut pec. A pebbled nipple.

Her other hand slid up his thigh. Brushed against the swell of his manhood. Hesitated. Opened, and cupped him in her palm.

Heat.

Life.

Love.

Startled, she opened her eyes and saw Mike staring down at her from their wedding picture, a sad acceptance turning his beloved face desolate.

"Stop." Julie scrambled to pull away, righting her clothes and trying not to cry. What had she done?

Connor eased back, confusion and then worry turning his eyes a stormy gray. "Talk to me, Jules." He reached out to brush her cheek and she flinched. He froze, and his hand fell to his lap. "What's wrong?"

Her gaze skittered. "Nothing. I just think we should focus on the case, that's all." She hopped to her feet and strode to the window, desperate to put some space between them.

"Jules."

She swung around, incensed. "Don't *call* me that. It's Julie, okay?"

Connor sat, gaze narrowed, under their wedding picture, and it was too much.

She hurried down the hall and into the washroom, tears blinding her path. The door slammed. Alone, with only her guilty eyes staring from the mirror for companionship, she slid to the floor and wept.

***

What the hell just happened?

Connor shook his head and rubbed the back of his neck, perplexed. They'd been enjoying each other's company—a lot—when Jules... Julie, suddenly spooked and high-tailed it out of the room like a scalded cat.

He needed to talk to her, apologize, but first he had to cool down. She'd managed to turn him inside out with just a few rubs and kisses. What would've happened if they had gone all the way? He shuddered.

She confused him more than any woman he'd ever met. What was it about her that wouldn't allow him to walk away? She was a distraction he couldn't afford right now. His job was to keep her safe and catch a murderer.

That's all she could be to him. A means to an end.

A cold blast hit him between the shoulder blades. He cursed, and turned, expecting to see the door flung wide, but it was still closed. Frowning, he stood and searched the room, grimacing at the knife-like pain in his back. The bright and cheerful room had turned gloomy, as though a storm brewed, though the sky beyond the window, was blue. His gaze landed on the disapproving face of Julie's dead husband. He tipped his head. It had to be a trick of lighting. The guy had been about to marry the most beautiful woman in the world, no way would he be pissed off.

Sure enough, when he moved so that the shadows dispersed, the picture went back to normal, a young couple, madly in love on their wedding day. It suddenly dawned on him what was wrong. Julie felt guilty. There was no reason to, her husband had been gone for some time now, but that wouldn't make it any easier.

Shit. He was an idiot.

Who else would make a move on a woman under her husband's watchful eyes?

He'd better apologize to her and hope like hell he hadn't ruined things between them forever. But first... "I'm sorry, man, but you had her love. How about giving me a chance?"

Connor sighed and turned away from her ex's condemning eyes drilling a hole in his back. Time to make a confession.

CHAPTER TWENTY-FIVE

Mike was having one of the worst days of his life. Okay, not true. Dying in a horrifying car crash topped the list, but still… His head hurt like a son-of-a-bitch, thanks to underestimating his guest's desire to escape. And now this.

He glared at the detective's retreating back. The idiot didn't deserve Jules. He didn't understand her at all. She was sweet, sensitive, innocent. A goddess on a pedestal. Not an easy lay on a Saturday afternoon.

But she cared about him.

Mike had seen it in her eyes. Something that gave him hope. And broke his heart. She was letting him go, moving on with her life.

He wanted her to be happy, but with a cop? That had late nights and endless worry written all over it.

What's the matter with an accountant or a lawyer, Jules?

Someone who wasn't going to leave her and the boys to fend for themselves. The way he had.

The cop softly knocked on the washroom door and rested his forehead on the wood. Mike's shoulders eased. The guy was into her, and it was more than just attraction. Mike could almost see the waves of regret rolling off his back. Maybe he did get her, after all.

The door opened and Jules stood on the threshold, her face pale and streaked with tears. The cop said a few words, reached out and brushed her cheek with his thumb, then gently tugged her into his arms.

Uncomfortable with the intimacy, as he hadn't been with their kissing, Mike zapped himself out of there.

He landed near the Transition House and cursed when he saw Lucas rising from the steps.

"Don't start with me, man. It's a bad time."

Lucas snorted. "Is there ever a good time for you, Monk?"

Mike ignored the jab. Lord knows why pretty boy decided to call him such a stupid name. "What are you doing here. Shouldn't you be off saving lives, or something?"

Lucas grinned. "Not without you, buddy. We're a team, remember?"

How could he forget? The Lord, in all his wisdom, had stuck the two of them together after the accident, the transgressor and the victim. A match made in Heaven.

"Don't remind me," he grumbled. Then it struck him, why was Lucas being nice? The last time they saw each other, they'd damn near come to blows. "What's going on? Why are you so cheerful?"

Lucas clapped him on the back and steered him toward the house. "No reason. I just figured if you can't beat 'em, join them, right? You'll tell me where Natalya is when you're ready, and me pissing you off isn't going to help with that." They trudged up the stairs together and Lucas waved him in first. "Think of it as turning over a new leaf."

Mike opened his mouth to impart a snarky comeback, but froze when he saw who awaited them inside.

"My Lord," he murmured, his soul filling with a mix of awe and shame. How was he going to explain his abduction of the girl to his Savior?

"Enter, my child. It has been too long." He sat on the sofa in front of the very fireplace where Natalya had fallen and bumped her head all those months ago. His snowy white robes flowed loosely around him, a foil for the long Santa Claus beard and shoulder-length hair. Startling blue eyes regarded him with nothing but warmth and compassion, ramping up his guilt to near claustrophobic proportions.

"Make room for your brother," the Lord said in his smooth baritone.

Mike glared over his shoulder, but Lucas just shrugged, obviously as surprised by their company as he was. They trudged into the room and took up a post on either end of the fireplace. Mike crossed his arms, then dropped them to his sides, uncomfortable under Father's knowing gaze.

"Does this visit mean we're finally moving on from this pit?" Lucas, ever the mouthpiece, was the first to speak.

The Lord's quiet stare was enough to make him hang his head. "Forgive me, Sire."

"You're an idiot," Mike said.

Lucas snorted. "Takes one to know one, doesn't it?"

Fire flared between them, the sparks angrily leaping from the hearth.

"Enough." The Savior's tone wasn't loud, but still it shouted his condemnation into the room.

Mike sank to his knees, overwhelmed. Why did he always let Lucas get to him?

"I thought you two would learn to get past your differences." Father said, his expression ripe with disappointment. "To forgive one another."

Mike glanced at Lucas, prayed that he'd keep his mouth shut about Natalya. "We're working on it."

"Well, you'll have another opportunity," Father said. "You will soon be called upon to help the people you care about on earth." His radiant blue gaze traveled from Lucas to Mike. "You will have to work together or bear the consequences. There's only one way to the other side, my children." He held out aged hands, hands that carried the weight of the world. "You must learn to love one another. For without love, there is no hope."

A ray of such warmth and light radiated from the Lord's hand into Mike's his vision blurred. Chest swelling with emotion, his mind filled with images of his family.

Please God, let them stay safe.

CHAPTER TWENTY-SIX

An earthquake could have hit the island and it wouldn't have caused as much upheaval as Julie was feeling at this moment. She rested her cheek against the cool porcelain of the bathtub and closed her aching eyes. Her throat hurt from fighting to hold back the emotions ripping their way up her esophagus. The last thing she needed was Connor coming to check on her.

As if he heard her silent plea, a knock came on the door and his voice pleaded, "Let me in, baby. I just want to make sure you're okay." It was silent for a moment and Julie held her breath, hoping he'd leave. But of course he didn't. "Please, honey."

Giving in to the inevitable, she rose and turned on the tap, keeping her gaze on the sink and the water going down the drain. Sighing, she bowed her head and rinsed her face, then let the coolness pour over her wrists. He deserved an explanation, she just didn't know what she was going to say. "Oh sorry, I thought you were my husband." Somehow, she didn't think that would be well-received. And besides, it wasn't true.

There was no mistaking Connor for anyone except himself. And that was the problem. For the first time in over a decade she was attracted to another man and wasn't sure how to handle her feelings.

When some of her hard-won composure returned, Julie turned off the water, dried her hands, and strode to the door. She grasped the handle, but couldn't quite bring herself to let him in yet.

"You must think I'm an idiot," she murmured.

His voice was warm, coaxing. "Then we can be idiots together. I'm sorry, Julie. I need my head examined. I'd never do anything to knowingly hurt you. You know that, right?"

She leaned her forehead on the smooth wood. "You didn't hurt me," she whispered.

There was a rough sigh from the other side. "Good. I was afraid I'd scared you away."

Slowly, she eased the door open. Connor stood in the frame, one lean forearm resting near her head. He looked at her as though searching for answers she couldn't give, then his mouth ticked up in a near-smile.

"Hi," he said.

Her heart fluttered like a hummingbird's wings. The man was devastatingly handsome. She couldn't believe he didn't have a bevy of beauties lined up waiting for his attention. Or maybe he did. The thought repelled and then she immediately kicked herself. She wasn't ready to step up to the plate, but lo and behold anyone who was. She shook her head, amused.

"What's so funny?" he asked, his head tipping quizzically.

Before she thought better of it, Julie reached up and brushed that stubborn lock of auburn hair, her fingers lingering to massage the lines from his brow.

She lost herself in the liquid depths of his eyes, shades of blue-gray like the softest of spring rains.

"Julie…"

"Shh," she whispered. "Just let me…"

She leaned forward and teased his lips with hers. Light, feathery kisses designed to tantalize. Taste. Torment.

He groaned, low in his chest, and the vibration sent goosebumps of desire rippling across her skin. The kisses grew deeper, more passionate. Tongues and teeth vied for position. He took over, his body pressing her back against the door. His hand captured both of hers and pinned them above her head. His knee between her legs and the friction of his thigh frustrated even as it excited.

He left her lips and she moaned, a cry that turned into gasps of pleasure when his tongue found her breast. She tugged on her hands, wanting, needing to touch him. To drive him as crazy as he was driving her. He released her to glide down to the hem of her shirt, then hesitated. Waited for her response.

A warm surge moved through her chest. He cared about her. This wasn't just some quick lay, filled with a morning after of regrets. What was happening between them was new—fresh. It had nothing to do with the past. They were both single, healthy adults. Who happened to have the hots for each other.

She reached down and with one quick tug, the t-shirt came off, leaving her bare from the waist up except for the hot flush suffusing her chest. A sudden case of embarrassment had her covering her breasts with her hands.

Connor's gaze warmed her further, the heated appraisal a benediction for her battered ego. It was a long time since a man looked at her that way. Mike had loved her body, but with two kids, a mortgage, and an ever-growing stack of bills, their love-life had often gone by the wayside.

Connor nibbled her fingers, scattering her thoughts like confetti. She stared at his dark head and something dangerous moved within her breast. This man could hurt her. He was driven, at times arrogant and bossy, but she'd seen his concern after his partner was hurt and the anger and regret for the women who had been murdered. He genuinely cared about the people under his watch.

"What are you thinking?" he asked, his lips nibbling her jaw.

She smiled. "How far it is to the bedroom."

That got his attention.

He lifted her chin and searched her eyes. "Are you sure? We don't have to go any further." His gaze moved down her body and turned wry. "I'll survive—somehow."

"I'm a woman, we change our minds. Do you want to stay or not, O'Rourke?"

Before she could second guess, he ducked and lifted her over his shoulder in a fireman's lift, his hand across her thighs holding her in place. "Which way?"

She snorted and ran her hands down his broad, muscled back. "Time's wasting. You're the detective, I'm sure you can figure it out."

He smirked and patted her bottom. She screeched and laughed, more light-hearted than she'd been in a very long time.

CHAPTER TWENTY-SEVEN

The aroma of fresh-brewed coffee brought Julie out of a deep sleep. She lay sprawled across her queen-sized bed, the covers helter-skelter except for the throw that normally resided on the wide ledge under the window. Connor must have covered her before he left the room.

Connor.

She closed her eyes, stretched like a well-fed cat, and buried her nose in the pillow that still smelled of him. Her body hadn't been her own last night. How else to account for this delicious ache between her thighs? The tender abrasions on her neck and breasts? And if he offered, she'd do it again. In a heartbeat.

A surprised laugh bubbled up her throat. She had never considered herself a wanton, but O'Rourke definitely knew his way around a woman's body. He'd done things that made her even now shiver with delight.

Maybe this was just what she needed—an affair with a nice, safe guy. A man who had *no entanglements* written all over him. That way she couldn't get hurt, and neither would he. It was all fun and games. At least until her kids came home.

Sobering, she climbed out from under the blanket and raced for the bathroom. It was one thing to think about an affair, and another for him to see her naked. She knocked lightly and was relieved to find the room empty. He must be in the kitchen then—or maybe he'd left.

Her stomach dropped. No, he wouldn't leave without a word. Would he?

She hesitated on the threshold, debating whether to call his name or not, then squared her shoulders and climbed into the shower. If he had left, it was fine. They had no commitment, he could do what he wanted.

Her skin burned with a mixture of hurt and embarrassment. She stood under the cleansing spray and let the sponge drop to the floor of the tub. Who was she kidding? She couldn't do this. She couldn't have sex without caring about the other person, and caring led to… other things. She wasn't ready to move in that direction, maybe she'd never be ready. Mike had occupied such a large place in her heart for so very many years, how could she consider shoving him aside now?

She tipped shampoo into her palm and rubbed her hands together to build up suds before applying it to her hair. She should get it cut. Mike had always urged her to keep it long, he'd liked running his fingers through the strands, but she preferred it shorter, easier to care for.

The therapist had warned her to take her time, everyone approached the grieving process differently. She understood that. Dustin had treated it with anger, Freddy with confusion. Mike's parents still went to the graveyard every Sunday and laid bouquets of his favorite tiger lilies in front of the gravestone. Julie had gone also, at first. But the more the Crenshaws tried to make peace with his loss—and baby Ava, buried with her daddy at that cement marker, the further away Julie wanted to run. That wasn't her family under six feet of black topsoil. Her husband was no doubt fishing the streams dry in Heaven while Ava made daisy necklaces on the bank. That's the way she wanted to picture them. Much as she loved being close to both sets of parents, she had decided to leave the past behind. It was just her and the boys now, and slowly but surely they were learning to function as a family again.

She tipped her head and let the water sluice the soap away along with her doubts. She was overthinking—again. If Connor was willing, an affair was just what the doctor ordered. It was time she set the grief aside and began to enjoy life again.

The door opened behind her and she smiled. And what better way than with a little water sports?

***

Connor opened the shower stall and almost swallowed his tongue. Julie had a black rose tattooed on her hip. It was a stark contrast to the alabaster skin on her butt and the smooth line of her slender back. She reminded him of Eve in the Garden of Eden. Beautiful. Impossible to resist. And when she glanced over her shoulder with those golden-brown eyes, he was drawn into her web, a willing captive.

"I made coffee," he murmured, and picked up an oval bar of soap to glide over her back; shoulder to shoulder, neck to waist, with a little extra attention spent on that intriguing tattoo.

"Mmm," she hummed. His dick leaped in response. "I smelled that. You're very… resourceful, detective."

He was totally onboard with that appraisal. There were things he could do with a bar of soap that a marketing company could make a fortune with for the right audience. He planned on perfecting his technique on a couple of those maneuvers today.

He moved closer, nibbling her neck while the soap did a slip and slide over a hip to explore the womanly curve of her stomach before bumping its way up her ribcage to the swell of her breast.

"You're so beautiful," he whispered, his gaze intent on the ever-narrowing circle he was creating in his quest to reach her nipple. It was dusky rose, a perfect match for lips opened in a little *ooh* that told him better than any spoken word how much he affected her. He loved her sensuality, and marveled that she didn't know how attractive she was. In many ways she seemed innocent, untouched, and yet—their time together last night had blown his mind.

Her hand moved to cover her breast and he nudged it aside. "Don't. I want to look at you." He turned her around so that he could better see her face. "Am I going too fast for you?" God, he hoped not. The last thing he wanted was to scare her off.

She shook her head and met his gaze with a trace of embarrassment. "My body isn't a twenty-year-old's anymore. I just don't want to disappoint you."

His heart clenched. Is that what she thought?

Her gorgeous eyes stared at him, and the water beading along the lashes made them appear dipped in stardust. The faint smattering of freckles across the bridge of her nose invited kisses, and the downy softness of her cheeks begged his touch.

No, she wasn't twenty. She was a woman with a siren's body. One that called to him with a song he couldn't resist.

"Do I look disappointed?" He invited her to see the effect she had on him.

One glance and her cheeks turned rosy. Her fingers hovered, and his breath backed up his throat.

"May I?" she asked, peeping up at him through those wet lashes.

"God, yes," he said, choking.

The hesitant touch of her fingers was the single most erotic sensation he'd ever felt. His hands clenched as she explored his length.

Teasing.

Provocative.

Soul destroying.

He fought against the overwhelming need to beg— and then she sank to her knees and he lost his mind.

CHAPTER TWENTY-EIGHT

He awoke with a crick in his neck and the sun burning a hole in his eyelids. He sat up and pawed at the visor, cursing. Still blurry-eyed, he glared at the house down the street.

She'd let the bastard spend the night, the whore.

An old lady walked toward him dragging a yappy Chihuahua by the leash. She slowed and stared suspiciously, probably because his windows were half fogged from being closed up all night. He turned the key to auxiliary, rolled his window down, and spit on the sidewalk.

That got her moving. She gave him a death-ray glare and tugged her pooch to the other side of the street.

He grinned, but the smile disappeared when his gaze resettled on the house. It was tempting to light the thing on fire and watch them burn, but that would only give him a momentary pleasure, it wasn't enough. He needed her to see his face, fear what he planned to do to her—and the screams. That was the part he liked the most. Their cries proved he was the boss, superior to them in every goddamn way.

He looked down at his hands strangling the steering wheel and forced himself to relax. He took a drink from the cold cup of coffee he'd been nursing all night and grimaced. It tasted like shit, but at least it was wet. He ran a finger down the side of the red cup and smiled. His collection was growing. He'd made a game out of stealing fragments of his victims' lives and watching them wonder what was going on. Then, when he had them in his grasp, he'd lay the pieces out around their prone bodies and they'd know... It would be there in the dilation of their pupils, in the tensing of already tense muscles, in the surge of panic-driven thrashing. He'd been stalking them long before they were taken—if only they'd paid attention to the signs.

He could have told them it wouldn't have mattered—they were women. Inferior beings. Good for cleaning and fucking and not much else. Certainly not worthy of raising children. Look at his own mother—may she burn in Hell—the bitch had done everything in her power to belittle him from the time he learned to walk. It hadn't mattered what he tried to do to please her, it always fell short. He pictured her laid out on that table, gasping for breath, and his chest swelled with pleasure. He'd enjoyed making her beg for mercy. It had felt incredibly good. All-empowering. The release from years of abuse was heady. He'd gone wild for a time, partying, traveling, doing whatever he wanted, whenever he wanted.

The sex came easily, women had always found him attractive. He'd even managed a couple of *normal* relationships, that is until the woman in question decided to create rules. He hated rules, refused to ever be bound by them again. Freaking broads, never knew when to leave a guy alone. They always needed everything cut and dried.

"The lawn needs mowing, honey."

"Could you be a sweetheart and take out the trash?"

"Why can't you ever pick up after yourself? Just because you're a cripple, do you think I'm your maid?"

That one had been the first to die—after his dear old mom. She'd hit a nerve, and before he knew what he was doing, her neck had snapped and her eyes had rolled back in her too-stupid-to-live head. The anger had been all-encompassing. So she thought of him as a cripple, did she? He'd left her lying in a puddle of her own urine, gone out to the garage, and came back with a hacksaw. It took some doing, but he'd managed. Now she could travel through Hell the way he did on earth—with one goddamn foot.

Instead of remorse, it was relief that flooded his gut and put a smile on his lips. Dumb bitch.

He'd wrapped her in a blanket, carefully removed any sign of his presence, and took her on a one-way drive to the forest. It had been surprisingly easy to get away with. Even when their connection came out in the investigation, his job had given him an airtight alibi.

After that he'd avoided relationships, turning to one-night stands and prostitutes to take care of business. But something was always missing. Nothing gave him the same thrill he'd felt taking a life. And that's when he turned his fantasies into reality. His travels gave him a wide-open hunting ground, here today, gone tomorrow. The cops never even came close to catching up, so he decided to up the stakes, leave them some clues. Not enough to find him, he wasn't that stupid, but just enough to make the game worth playing.

He thought of the thrill he got from branding that first bitch, the stench of singed flesh, the screams of pain. Better than drugs. The rush of power flew through every atom of his body, zinging like lightning through his blood, filling his pores, and making his cock swell. He was always careful, no need to leave any DNA for the cops to find, and when he was done, he'd end their pitiful lives. Snuff out their hopes and dreams the same way his had been killed. Show them how weak they were. How stupid.

A car pulled into the driveway and sat idling. A moment later O'Rourke stepped out the door, followed by Julie. He lifted his hand to acknowledge the driver, then turned and pulled her into his arms, right there in broad daylight. The bitch had her claws in him good. That's okay, it wouldn't be for long.

O'Rourke kissed her, then waited until she went inside before getting into the squad car. Too bad he didn't realize it was too late—trouble had already found its way to the Crenshaw house.

CHAPTER TWENTY-NINE

Connor had a tough time holding his goofy smile inside. He couldn't remember ever feeling like this—lighthearted, happy. Filled with promise. Julie was amazing. Warm, beautiful, smart. By mutual agreement, they'd left their troubles at the door and spent twenty-four hours in their own little world, no past, no future, just now. He liked her—a lot. She was funny, sweet, and incredibly sexy. He wanted more time with her before the kids returned and life got complicated. And they still needed to talk. He wanted her to give up the ABC Killer story, it was getting too dangerous. The prick was playing with them. It was almost like he knew their moves before they did.

"You're looking pretty pleased with yourself," Maddie said.

Connor glanced over, pulled out of his thoughts. "Where's Matt?" He ignored her knowing look, concern furrowing his brow. "I thought he was back on shift?"

She signaled and took the corner before answering him. "He was, then he called in yesterday afternoon and booked out, said his head was hurting."

Damn. Matt was his partner; he should have been there for him. Make sure he got his stubborn ass into the doctor's. He pulled his cell out of his pocket and checked for messages. Nothing. Matt had no family. Over the years, Connor had taken on the role of older brother—read listener, slash guidance counselor. They'd butted heads a few times, but had grown close, too. Connor couldn't ask for a better guy to have at his back.

He speed-dialed Matt's number, but got the answering machine. "Hey, bro, give me a call, we have work to do." He clicked off and shrugged at Maddie's enquiring look. If Matt didn't get back to him by the end of the day, he'd pop over and check on him. For now, he had a case to catch up on.

"What's happening with our Jane Doe?" he asked.

He could see her donning her police mantle, it almost made him smile. He'd been that young once, idealistic. Years of fighting a losing battle with crime and corruption had leeched the naiveté out of him like a vampire sucks blood. It had left him jaded, cynical. Until Julie. She made him feel young again, like anything was possible.

"No news on the body yet, sir, they're still looking. There's a lot of old growth forest to comb through, not to mention the rivers and ravines. They've brought in the cadaver dogs, but she could be anywhere." Maddie slowed to a stop for a red light and turned to meet his gaze. "Vancouver, sir, that's a lot of people to protect." The light turned green and she continued down the road, the silence oppressive.

She was right. They were up against nearly insurmountable odds. The prick could be anywhere between the mainland and here. For all they knew, he could be holed up on one of the Gulf Islands right now, just a ferry hop away from his next victim.

He stared out the front window, absently noting the arrival of spring evident in the budding cherry and magnolia trees lining the road, the lush green of the grass, and the city's landscapers out en masse preparing for the busy tourist season. Just another reason why he needed to catch this guy—and soon.

They pulled up to the station a short time later. Connor was relieved to see his car in the parking lot, retrieved from the airport as per his request. He nodded toward it, glancing at the corporal, "Did you see to that?"

She stopped beside him and he was faintly surprised by her lack of height, barely clearing his shoulders. Her forceful personality within the walls of the office more than made up for any lack of stature.

"I did," she answered. "It's also been filled up, washed, and the interior cleaned, sir."

He acknowledged her unspoken reprimand. "Thank you, corporal. I appreciate you taking the time and effort." He headed for the doors, but couldn't resist one last jab. "Next time, try and park it in my stall."

She was still sputtering when he pulled the door open, waited for clearance, and then strode toward his office. But once the door closed, he sobered. A quick call through to the Vancouver PD verified everything Maddie had told him, with the addition of new evidence—the search team had uncovered a small chest filled with assorted items, including a puzzle piece. The other articles included a watch, a locket containing a child's portrait—his heart tugged—and a pair of non-prescription reading glasses. It was like the bastard was taunting them.

They had unearthed a similar chest near the woman found in Sooke. What was his game? Why the puzzle pieces? And why did he take mementoes of their lives only to stash them with the bodies? It must have some sort of significance for him, like the severing of the feet. Connor's gut was telling him this guy was either an amputee, or had been abused by one. It made sense. He'd probably been bullied— most likely by a woman he had counted on for love and support, either a parent or a lover.

Connor grabbed a pen and paper to write down his synopsis.

A tradesman- someone who frequently traveled.

Mid-thirties-early forties- Had to be in decent shape due to location of the victims.

Handicapped- Either himself or someone close to him.

A loner- His disconnect feeds his aggression. Don't discount marriage, but unlikely.

Knowledge of the area- has a working knowledge of the coastal areas.

And maybe the most important-

Has knowledge of police procedures.

Connor turned on his computer and started an inter-departmental search for one or more hits off his list. While he waited, he leaned back in his chair and contemplated the far wall. His wall of pride, he'd called it. There was the framed portrait of him graduating police academy—The Depot—in Regina. Various commendations and awards, and even a picture of him and his wife, Carla, taken not long before she'd been killed on the job. He'd known marrying a fellow officer, even if she was from another department, was a risk. Their lives were on the line twenty-four-seven, it was just part of the job. But he'd always figured he'd be the one to go, never her. It had devastated him for a long time.

Long enough to wonder if he wasn't making a mistake getting tangled up with Julie.

The women in his life didn't fare very well.

CHAPTER THIRTY

Julie floated down the hall to her bedroom. The past hour shimmered in her mind like an erotic film noir. The tough, cynical detective and the lonely widow. She grinned like a love-struck fool. Connor brought out her inner rebel. She'd taken the lead in the shower for the very first time in her life—and she'd liked it.

He'd received a call for work not long after, so they hadn't had much time to talk, but Connor had mentioned taking her out for dinner later. That seemed promising.

She opened the drawer and dug through until she came out with some spicier underclothes than her usual comfort wear. Might as well dress to impress, just in case. Her eyes shined at her in the mirror, betraying her anticipation. She fingered the slight rash on her neck, a visual reminder of the man and all the places that mouth had been.

She hugged the memories close.

Whatever happened from here on out, Connor had given her a gift. He'd proven with his loving and kisses that instead of a dried up old widow at the age of twenty-nine, she was still a woman—and a sensual one too.

She was buttoning her blouse over a pair of gray linen pants when the doorbell rang. Her heart stuttered and her fingers missed the hole.

He came back.

She finished fastening her shirt, tucked it into her slacks, took a last glance in the mirror, noted her flushed cheeks, and hurried down the hall to open the door.

"What did you forget?" The laughter sputtered out when she tugged the door open and saw who was on the other side.

"Hey," Ron said, his gaze doing an appraising head-to-toe before coming back to her face. "Thought

I'd stop by and see if you wanted to go over our notes."

Julie bit back a retort. He could have waited the ten minutes for her to get to the station. She immediately felt bad. It wasn't his fault she'd been hoping her lover had returned. Imagine that, she had a lover.

The goofy grin returned and Ron smiled in reply, stepping past her into the house.

"You're in a good mood today. What happened, you get laid?"

She stiffened. How could he know that?

He glanced at her over his shoulder as he set a pile of folders onto the coffee table. "I'm kidding, sheesh. It was a joke, Crenshaw. You going to help me with these, or what?"

She reluctantly closed the door and followed him into the room. "You don't need to be a pig, Ron. Let's just stick with the case, shall we?"

He shrugged and sat in the same chair Connor had occupied, but whereas he'd seemed rather adorably uncomfortable, Ron sat back and crossed one long leg to rest his ankle over his knee.

"Yeah, sure, whatever. I've been compiling all this shi… stuff while you were away. Boss wants to run with the story for the weekend edition so we gotta roll."

Guilt mixed with annoyance. This was her story. She didn't mind sharing the spotlight with the rest of her team, but since when did that include Ron? Still, it was good of him to gather the info and bring the files over. He could have left her out of the loop and gone straight to Taylor, taking all the credit.

"Thanks, Ron. I do appreciate your input on this. How about a peace-offering? Would you like a cup of coffee?" She wasn't sure if the satisfied gleam in his eye came from her compliance or the thought of caffeine.

"Yeah, that would be great. I haven't had my quota yet today." He grinned and that attractive dimple made an appearance. "I'll sort these out while you get it ready."

She nodded and turned away. She needed to cut him some slack. He really was a nice guy.

***

A couple of hours later they had ironed out a presentation that Taylor would love. It was sensationalist journalism at its finest—great for reviews, not as good for peace of mind.

Julie's research had shown a trail of death that swept from one end of the country to the other over the course of a decade, and yet the RCMP hadn't picked up on the similarities until the past year. Or at least not that they were admitting to. Part of the problem was the killer's MO. He'd changed over the years, become more refined. Colder. The first murders were the work of rage. The forty-five-year-old choked until it ruptured capillaries in her eyes and nose and crushed her trachea. Then there was the young mother, savagely raped and murdered, her foot cut off with a hacksaw.

Who did something like that to another human being?

She shuddered and turned the page of the report. After that everything got quiet for a while. Maybe he'd traveled, maybe even gone to prison on another offense, there was no way to tell until they caught him, but then, it happened again.

This time it was Winnipeg, and the woman was a street worker. Aboriginal, sixteen, missing from her home for a year and a half before the body was found dumped in a farmer's well. Missing a foot.

Since then there had been at least five more cases she could attribute to the ABC Killer as he'd worked his way west. Now he was on their turf and she planned on doing whatever she could to bring him down.

Whether Connor approved or not.

"Listen," Ron interrupted her musing. "I think we should take another drive out to Sooke, talk to some of the townsfolk and get more of the human interest angle. What do you think?"

Julie nodded. It would look good on TV, the distraught parents, the overworked mayor trying to control her town's very real fears. It was a less than agreeable part of the job, but necessary for ratings. She understood, but she didn't have to like it.

"You can do the interviews. I'll be your cameraman for the day. Unless you think we should wait for Sam and Rudy?" he asked, rising to his feet. He was a big man and she hurried to stand to gain a more level footing.

"I'm sure we can manage," she said, and grabbed her purse from the floor. "Let's get going then. I want to be back in time to add this to the post."

Something flashed in his eyes, too quick for her to catch, then the killer smile was back and he raised a hand to guide her out the door. "After you."

CHAPTER THIRTY-ONE

Julie kept both hands on the wheel, uncomfortable with driving Ron's four-by-four truck on the narrow, winding road to Sooke. When he'd mentioned the start of a headache she'd offered to drive, but had expected to be using her Civic, not his big boy toy. He wanted to get some shots of the forestry trunk road where the victim had been found, and though her car might be cute, she knew its limitations.

Marshmallow clouds layered the horizon, creating an intimate setting in the cab that would have been great with Connor—with Ron...not so much.

"I hope we can get back to town before the rain starts," she said, glancing over to see him thumbing over map coordinates on his cellphone. "What's the matter? I thought you said you knew where we were going?"

He gave her a crooked smile. "I said I *thought* I knew where we were going. I'm new to the island too, don't forget. Still learning my way around. Don't worry," he held up his phone, "Siri will lead us the right way."

She grimaced and turned her attention back to the road. Just what she needed, missing in the boonies all day. Connor would be upset. She should call him before she lost cell coverage—it had been spotty the last time she'd been to Sooke.

She felt around on the seat beside her and came up empty-handed. What the…? A quick glance told her what she already knew—her purse was missing.

She glared at Ron. "Who told you to move my purse? Give it back. What if the kids need me?"

He gave her a *what-the-fuck* look that made her feel like she'd taken Freddy's last stick of bubblegum for no good reason.

"Relax, jeez. It's on the floor. I'm sure we'll hear if your phone rings." He shook his head and went back to reading maps, but she noticed he didn't set her bag back on the seat either.

Men. They'd do something that made no sense and when you called them on it, they'd invariably get defensive. She turned down the radio to a dull roar, grimacing at his taste in music. Punk rock, really? No wonder he had a headache. And Connor thought she was bad.

"So spill the beans, Henderson. Where are you from? Ever been married? Kids?" Julie was surprised by how little she knew about him considering they'd been working together for the past six months, ever since Ron joined the station.

He looked up from his phone, one eyebrow giving her the high five. "Wow, Crenshaw, that's some mean reporting skills you got going there."

He rolled his window halfway down, giving them a cool blast of spring. "Ontario, no, and no. Does that answer your questions?" Then, before she could come up with a snooty answer he threw them back at her. "What about you? I know your husband died." She flinched. "And you have two boys, but where did you come from? What made you decide to become a reporter? Why here?"

Served her right for being nosy.

She shot him a sideways glance, saw his genuine interest, and dialed back her retort. "We both came from Chicago. I loved it there, the city is beautiful, vibrant, but Mike's dream had always been to move here, to the island."

She rubbed her wedding ring as though it were a lucky talisman. "We spent our honeymoon here and decided this was the perfect place to raise children." She gave him a wry twist of the lips. "You know what they say about best laid plans…" She shrugged. "Anyway, Chicago wasn't the same without Mike."

He reached over and patted her leg. "Sorry, kid."

She blinked away the annoying tears and shifted her knees closer together, uncomfortable until he removed his hand. There was an awkward silence, broken only by the howling of his off-road tires chewing up the pavement.

"Hey, I hope you don't think I was hitting on you, or anything." He laughed. "You're not exactly my type, if you know what I mean."

She relaxed, smiling. "Not young enough, right?"

He stared at her, all indignant-like. "What are you trying to say, Crenshaw? My dates are all legal-aged."

"Yeah?" she quipped. "By how much?"

He snorted. "Jealous?"

"Ha. First I'd have to like you, Ron." She blinked at him innocently.

"Touché." He acknowledged her jab. "I'll have to work on that, then."

A few fat splats on the windshield heralded the arrival of the rain. Julie searched the levers until she figured out how to switch the wipers on. Why couldn't they make every vehicle the same?

"Hope this is just a shower," she said, peering up at the fast-moving mass of gray above their heads.

Ron rolled up his window and flicked on the defrost. "Spring storms are unpredictable. I wouldn't worry though, ol' Betsy here will see us through." He lovingly patted the dash.

Hmm, for reporters they had a distressing lack of originality when it came to naming their cars.

"How long have you had her?" Julie asked, noticing the carefully polished chrome and spotless carpet.

Ron shrugged and fiddled with the radio. "I dunno, eight or ten years, I guess."

She glanced at the odometer, almost two hundred thousand clicks. He must keep it serviced regularly, it still ran whisper-quiet for a big vehicle.

"Don't let the boys in here." She nodded toward the worn, but clean seats. "They're little monsters with sticky hands."

He looked suitably worried. "Good to know."

He pointed toward a turn coming up on their right. "Here it is."

Julie slowed, clicked the turn signal on, and moved to the side of the road to allow the traffic behind room to go around. The road was gravel, as expected, and snaked upward into a tall stand of cedar and hemlock, so tall they seemed to shake hands with the clouds.

She drove for a couple of miles, both hands mangling the wheel, before glancing at Ron. "How far?"

He kept his eyes on the road. "Don't know. We should see some police tape or something when we get closer."

Sure enough, another couple of switchbacks later the reflective yellow of the tape fluttered on branches with the force of the wind. Julie shivered. The whole place carried a spooky, malevolent atmosphere. This high up, with the moisture coating the air, mist wove in and out of the trees like ghostly wraiths from some horror movie.

The body was gone, take to the Medical Examiner's office for analysis, but it still felt as though remnants of the murder remained.

The terror.

Desperation.

The rage.

It was impossible to understand what drove a person to commit such a heinous crime. Even taking into consideration the possibility of child abuse and all the ugly connotations that went with it, most people sought counseling and managed to live a somewhat normal life—even if it was never forgotten.

Not this guy.

He'd taken on the role of vigilante justice, at least in his own mind. It all made a twisted sort of sense to Julie. He saw these women as symbols of whoever hurt him in the past—and his focus was to make them pay. Which made her think he'd been helpless against the person who had injured him—wife? Parent? Whoever it was, they'd managed to create a monster and were just as guilty as he was, in her opinion.

"Ready?"

Ron's voice made her jump. She'd been so busy recreating events she'd forgotten he was there.

"Yes. Let's get our shots and get out of here. This place creeps me out." She shut off the truck's diesel engine, rubbed clammy hands on her trousers, and opened the door to jump down. She glanced over her shoulder as she slid off the seat to the ground and caught a look on Ron's face that almost froze her in mid-air.

Satisfaction.

What the hell was that about?

CHAPTER THIRTY-TWO

Connor sat up and stared at his computer screen.

You gotta be kidding me. He'd been right under their noses the entire frigging time. How had they missed this?

He shoved his chair away and paced to the door, flinging it back on its hinges, and striding down the hall, his heart pounding out a furious hurry, hurry before-it's-too-late. He dialed Julie as he walked. *C'mon, honey, be there, be there.*

No answer. *Fuck.*

Officers stared at him like startled deer, then stood and reached for their vests, no questions asked.

Not so Maddie. She turned from the file cabinet and hurried over. "What's wrong? Is it Matt?"

Connor hesitated, aware of her feelings for his partner. "Were you aware Matt transferred here from Ontario?"

She frowned. "No, why?"

"C'mon, I need to check on Julie. We can talk in the car." He waved the other officers back to their seats. "I'll call if I need you. Be ready to roll." He knew he came off sounding harsh, but worry had knotted his stomach until he could barely breathe. Visions of the woman at the morgue kept cycling through his mind, reminding him their unknown suspect was an unconscionable killer.

Maddie was already buckled in and waiting in the passenger seat of his car, and he silently thanked her for knowing he needed to do something, even if it was only to drive—for now. He couldn't even consider anything else. If that bastard had Julie… Connor would move Heaven and earth to find her.

"What's going on, sir? Why did you ask me about Matt?" Maddie hung on, her face grim.

He shot her a quick sideways glance, then focused on the road, the cruiser's red and blues bouncing their colors off the panes of glass as they flew down the business district.

"I ran an intensified search using the information we've gathered so far and came up with a hit." He laughed, but it wasn't with humor. "More than one, actually. There's been at least eight cases with direct links to our guy. Same MO, and we missed it." He shook his head. "I can't believe we missed it."

Maddie's gaze was stricken, "Matt? It can't be Matt. I went out with him. We were… close." She clenched her hands. "You're wrong about this, sir. Dead wrong."

He squeezed the life out of the steering wheel. "Yeah, well, let's hope you're right, or it might be Julie that's next." A cocktail mix of fury, betrayal, and dread swirled in his gut. The more he thought about it, the more the anger churned. The son-of-a-bitch had used the police force, his friends, everyone. The why of it didn't even matter anymore. All Connor gave a shit about was bringing the bastard in before anyone else got hurt.

Especially Jules.

God, why wasn't she answering her phone?

He rounded the final corner on squealing tires and raced for the end of the block, only slowing at the last minute in case Matt was holding Julie hostage in her house. The last thing he wanted was to back the guy into a corner. He was police-trained; he wouldn't go down without a fight.

And there his car was, parked under a giant willow, halfway hidden from the street. Maddie pointed and swiped moisture from her eyes. He knew how she felt. Right up until this moment, he'd hoped against hope that he was wrong.

He turned off his lights, grateful he'd chosen to come in on a silent approach instead of with bells ringing. They would have next to no advantages against the suspect—he couldn't think of him as Matt—so they had to do whatever they could to gain the upper hand.

He opened his door, and was stopped by the hand on his arm.

"I'm sorry, sir." Her pretty green-gold eyes swam with sorrow, and with determination. She was something, Madeline Tate.

"Me too, corporal. The best we can do now is bring him in and give him a fair trial. You with me?"

She nodded. "Where do you want me?"

Good girl.

He nodded toward the back of the house. "You go that way. Make sure he doesn't make a run for it. And Maddie," he murmured. "Don't take any chances."

Her eyes widened as she took in his meaning to use force if necessary. "Let's hope it doesn't come to that, sir."

Oh, he was.

As Connor edged his way down the street, he kept hoping. Maybe Julie had fallen asleep after he left and didn't hear her phone. *Even though she kept it nearby in case her children called.* Maybe she'd decided on another shower, this time alone. Or maybe she'd stepped outside to take out the trash and was invited to a neighbor's house for coffee.

Anything other than what he feared.

He drew his weapon when he neared Matt's car. A quick glance in the windows proved the vehicle to be empty. A take-out container from a popular fast food chain lay untouched on the passenger seat just waiting to be opened. Why would he buy food right before going after his prey? A closer inspection showed a full cup of Matt's favorite coffee sitting in the holder, also untouched. Something wasn't adding up here.

Every muscle tensed for action, he crept to the back end of the car and crouched, searching for whatever had his sixth sense going crazy. There was absolutely no movement anywhere. It was like a scene from the Twilight Zone. Abandoned toys, scudding clouds, whirling dust. If he were superstitious he'd be seriously weirded out.

The house was across the street. Unless he was going to creep all the way down the block to come up the other side, there was nothing for it, but to make a dash for the bushes lining Julie's driveway and pray like hell he wasn't seen.

A faint moan near his ear startled his concentration so much he lost his balance and would have fallen if not for a quick hand against the bumper to steady himself.

What the hell?

He took one last glance at the house, then hurried to the driver's door. Locked. There wasn't time for finesse, so he used the butt of his gun and tapped the window once, twice, third time lucky. It popped and a hole appeared large enough to get his hand in and release the door handle. He reached down beside the seat and pushed the lever to open the trunk, then rushed to the back before whoever was in there could get away.

He grabbed the trunk, kept his gun trained on the opening, and lifted the lid.

It took a moment for his adrenaline to slow enough so he could comprehend what he was seeing. Matt lay bound in a fetal position, a blood-stained red and white kerchief shoved in his mouth and tied at the back. His hands were likewise secured behind him with a plastic zip tie pulled so tight his fingers looked like swollen sausages.

His bruised eyes opened and he made that inhuman wailing sound again, and Connor jumped into action. He undid the cloth and yanked it down, relief that his friend was alive—and that he'd been horribly wrong about him—blurring his vision.

"Fuck, man, there's easier ways to become a hero."

Matt's laugh was hoarse, betraying his emotion. "I thought I was going to be meeting my maker this time for sure." Then, as Connor helped him out of the trunk, "Have I mentioned that I'm claustrophobic? It felt like a fricken coffin in there, man. Did you get him?"

Connor paused from sawing through the cord holding Matt's wrists. He swung his friend around, and had to brace him against the car so he wouldn't fall.

"Get who?" he demanded. "Who did this to you, Matt? And what the hell are you doing sitting in front of the Crenshaw house, anyway?"

Matt lunged away from the car and would have fallen to his knees if Connor hadn't lodged a shoulder in his chest to hold him back.

"Slow down and tell me what's going on." Connor panted. "Why were you parked in front of Julie's house? I was told you were off sick."

Matt gave one last push, then stood and turned his back. "Untie me, we don't have much time."

Connor frowned, frustrated with the non-answers he'd received thus far. "Not until you tell me what the fuck is going on. Who knocked you out and dumped you in the trunk? What does Julie have to do with this? And why the hell didn't you call me, I'm your fricken partner." The last was said in a growl made deadlier for its quiet tone.

Matt's shoulders slumped, but he waited until Connor cursed and began sawing at the ties to answer.

"After I got out of the hospital, I went back to that tattoo place. I was pissed that guy got the drop on me, and convinced Marko knew more than he was telling us." The ties let go and Matt groaned his relief. He turned and met Connor's gaze, rubbing his wrists.

"Turned out I was right. After a little… persuasion, Marko admitted he'd been paid for those sketches by a reporter. Three guesses who?"

CHAPTER THIRTY-THREE

Julie shrugged off the combination of eerie skies and Ron's less than circumspect attitude. She slid out of the truck and slogged through the damp undergrowth toward the crime scene. She tried not to dwell on what had occurred to bring them to this forest hideaway, but the oppressive silence and deepening shadows screamed of the recent violence. It was about as far from the friendly fern and moss trails she and the kids had traveled since coming to the island as it was possible to be.

A door slammed and she glanced back to see Ron following with that enigmatic smile tipping the lips many of his fans regularly swoon-tweeted about. She shook her head. He could have the notoriety, she was happy in the background, doing the investigative reporting that made her station one of the leaders in journalism. Their success was her success.

"Should get some great shots for the feature," Ron called out.

She whirled on him, angry he could be so callous. "Have a little respect, Henderson. A woman died here. It's not always about making you look good, you jerk."

He glared at her, his eyes glinting a weird fluorescent green in the shadows of the giant cedars. "What's your problem? Why do you think we're here, if not to get a story?" He loomed closer and she suddenly realized she was deep in the forest— alone—with a guy who out-weighed her by at least a hundred pounds and looked as though he could take on Sasquatch and win.

She took a couple steps backward and surreptitiously searched for something she could use as a weapon. Not that she would need a weapon. Ron was just making a point; she'd overreacted. It was this place; evil seemed to lurk behind the trunk of every tree. It didn't help that the branches were dripping with waving fronds of moss that hung from the maples and covered the hemlocks before eating its way over the forest floor. For someone used to the urban jungle of Chicago, it could be a little intimidating.

She forced a light laugh and waved a hand to encompass the terrain. "Sorry. This place just has me on edge." She moved reluctantly closer to the yellow tape. "Let's get this done, so we can get out of here, okay? I'll buy lunch."

She ducked under the tape, careful to stay away from the trampled area where the forensics team had taken their samples. It saddened her to think of who this woman might have been; a mother, someone's wife, a daughter. It wasn't fair her life had been treated like gum on the bottom of that monster's shoe. She decided when Connor found out who her family was, Julie would get the boys to make a nice drawing, maybe do some baking, and take it over to them. It wouldn't bring her back, but at least they'd know someone cared.

Her gaze skittered over the crushed ground near the base of a freshly gouged tree, the bark shredded and raw from rope burns, suggesting the woman's torture. She wiped away the ready tears and hoped their investigation would help the police catch this animal and put him behind bars for a very long time.

"If you stand where I am, we can pan the scene and show women how important it is not to travel alone." She held her hands up as though viewing through the lens of a camera.

"Yes, it's really rather foolish of them."

Julie froze. That wasn't Ron's sarcastic, and at this moment, infinitely endearing, voice. It was…

She swung around and her hands covered her mouth to hold back the involuntary scream. Rudy stood over Ron's body, a hunting knife covered in fresh blood held loosely at his side.

"Hello, Julie." His lips twisted in his familiar half-smile, the one she'd thought so cute. The one that made her envy Sam.

Oh my God, Sam.

Her gaze jumped from Ron to the surrounding forest, then back to Rudy. She was vibrating so hard her knees threatened to dump her in the dirt, but if that happened, she'd die. She could see it in his eyes. Why had she never noticed how close together they were? How terrifying?

"Di… Did you kill him?" Her voice wavered. *I'm so sorry, Ron.* This was her fault. Rudy had come for her, and Ron had possibly paid the ultimate price. His life.

Rudy nudged the body with the hiking boots she'd always teased him and Sam for wearing. "Nah, I don't think so, but he will die if he doesn't get help soon." His smile was pure evil. "Too bad that's not going to happen."

What was she going to do? The keys were in the truck—as long as Rudy hadn't removed them—but he was between her and the vehicle. Speaking of which, how did he get up here without their knowledge?

"Where's Sam? How did you get up here?" She had to keep him talking, it was her only chance. She didn't even have her phone because Ron had left her purse on the damn floor of his damn truck in the damn forest where there wouldn't be any damn cell coverage anyway.

Calm down.

Freaking out would only get her killed faster. And wasn't that an encouraging thought?

"Where's Sam, Rudy? Is she part of this sick little game?"

He shook his head and took a couple steps closer, the knife glinting even as the clouds began to weep, the drops hitting the leaves overhead and creating a fine mist that soaked them in seconds.

"Nah, she's not like *them*." He waved the blade toward the crumpled earth behind her. "They deserved what they got. Flaunting their bodies, thinking they're better than everyone else. Perfect." He spat the last word out, his gaze venomous. "They weren't so damn perfect when I finished with them."

Ron moaned and thrashed on the ground. Rudy glanced down, and Julie took her chance and ran, praying she could draw him from the wounded reporter and get away herself. The sobs made it hard to breathe past the fear clawing her stomach and turning limbs leaden. Branches slapped her in the face and yanked her hair, but nothing could slow her headlong flight. She heard Rudy yell and it spurred her on faster. Go. Go.

Her instinct was to race for the logging road, but then she'd be in the open, easy prey, so she delved deep into the forest, climbing, climbing, higher and higher. A quick glance over her shoulder showed she'd made the right decision. Though he favored those godforsaken hiking boots and all she wore were a pair of flimsy sandals, he was falling behind.

This was a nightmare.

They'd been friends.

God, he and Sam had even cared for Dustin and Freddy when she had to work late. She shuddered. Did Sam know? No, she wouldn't believe that. She couldn't.

Tears blinded her to a felled tree and she tripped over it, landing with a soft oomph in the damp moss on the other side. Julie lay there for a moment, stunned, before scrambling to her knees. She peered through disheveled strands of hair and moving shadows caused by the swaying trees and dark rain clouds. She couldn't see him anymore, but his presence pervaded the forest, a dark force weighing her down with dread and fear.

She was going to die out here, all alone. Who would tell her boys? They'd be orphans.

God, please don't do this to them. To me.

Leaves rustled behind her and she flipped to her back, hands raised to protect herself. A scream strangled her throat until she saw black dots before her eyes.

And an angel.

There was a freaking angel with huge gray wings floating above her prone body. Julie clutched her breast and fainted dead away.

CHAPTER THIRTY-FOUR

Lucas stared down at the woman at his feet and thanked the Lord he'd made it in time. He couldn't stand the thought of hurting this family again, especially her. He wondered if she remembered him at all. Oh, not as the grisly old taxi driver, but as the man who had taken away her husband and child. The man she'd gazed at with recrimination and horror as their vehicles raced toward a fatal collision there was no way to avoid.

Yeah, that guy.

She'd fainted just now when she'd seen him; a reaction he'd been used to achieving with his adoring fans… not so much since he became an angel.

He needed her to wake up, they didn't have a lot of time before her enemy arrived. The Lord had granted him and Mike a vision before they left Transition

House. The other angel had been understandably shaken; his wife was in mortal danger. They'd split up upon reaching earth in the hope of finding her before it was too late. God was probably laughing at fate right now. Lucas owed this family, and now it was time to pay.

He sank to earth and knelt beside her, saddened by the ravages her husband's death had placed upon her body. A shock of silver ran through her hair and deep lines carved the edges of her mouth into a perpetual grimace. Her body was more thin than lean, as though she ate only for nutrition, not enjoyment. He held her hand, the wedding ring loose on her finger, and rubbed warmth into rapidly cooling skin.

"Wake up, Mrs. Crenshaw." He waited a moment and when she didn't move, he tapped her cheek. "Julie, you need to wake up now. I need your help."

She moaned, just the softest little puff of air, then opened her eyes. When she saw him, they grew so big they encompassed her face. Her body went stiff just before she scrambled backward on her elbows, coming up hard against a fallen tree covered in moss the same soft green as her eyes.

"Who are you? What do you want?" Her gaze went to his now folded wings. "I'm dreaming, aren't I? You're a figment of my imagination."

She waved a trembling hand back and forth in front of her body. "All of this is. I'm going to wake up in my bed, in my freaking house, and this will all go away. Right? *Right*?"

Panic made her voice waver and Lucas wished like hell he could agree and take away her fear, but he couldn't. All he could do was save her life, and that was a vow he planned on keeping.

"Shh, you need to keep your voice down. There's a very bad man chasing you. Do you remember that?" He didn't mean to scare her, but they had to play this smart. He was still learning his capabilities. Now was not the time to find out his shortcomings.

She glanced over her shoulder—probably searching for said bad guy—then stared at him until he became uncomfortable.

"What? You can ask me anything," he said, hoping she wouldn't.

"Are you here because I'm going to die?"

"What? No," he exclaimed. "Nothing like that."

He stood and paced a couple of feet away, agitated by her matter-of-fact attitude to her possible demise. "Think of me as your guardian angel. I'm here to keep you safe. Your children need their mother, so don't you give up, okay?" Shit, did she *want* to die?

Where the hell was Mike? He'd know the right words, the ones she needed to hear.

"You have to be strong. Can you do that for me?"

She hesitantly nodded, and wiped the tears from her cheeks leaving smudges with fingers stained from the tumble she'd taken.

Relieved, Lucas held out his hand to help her up. She accepted, but pulled away as soon as she could, stumbling on the rough terrain. He glanced down and shook his head; who goes into the woods wearing sandals?

A crash from off to their left warned Lucas his time was running out. Julie looked ready to faint or flee—he wasn't sure which—and he needed her to know something before she did either, so he grasped her arm and ignored her outraged gasp.

"Listen. I want you to run downhill as quick as you can. Try to make it to the truck and get away." Her eyes were glazed with terror and he gave her a little shake. "Mrs. Crenshaw, do you hear me?" He turned her in the right direction and pushed. "Go. I don't know how much…"

She didn't wait to hear his warning, instead lighting out of there as though the hounds of hell were after her. And indeed, they were.

***

Julie flew down the hill, her feet barely touching the ground. Now that she had a goal, the shock subsided so that she could think. Not that she wanted to. It seemed incomprehensible that she could be fleeing a serial killer who just happened to be her best friend's husband. Seriously, horror movie you-just-can't-make-this-shit-up crazy.

And what about the angel?

No one was going to believe that one. She snorted. If she didn't make it, it wouldn't matter, there'd be no one left to tell the story. Well, except Rudy, but she didn't think he was talking.

How could she joke at a time like this? It was either that or lose her freaking mind, that's how. She glanced over her shoulder, but it was just a blur. In a far-off corner of her mind she understood that her body was in shock, everything she'd seen today playing out in a non-stop reel that kept adrenaline pumping through her veins. It was probably keeping her alive right now, giving super-human bursts of speed to legs that normally enjoyed a leisurely walk a heck of a lot more than an Olympic-type sprint through a heavily wooded forest.

More than once, she tripped and had to grab onto whatever was nearby to avoid kissing the ground again. Her knees still throbbed from the last fall. Though that was nothing compared to poor Ron. Was he still alive? There'd been so much blood. It churned her stomach, making it hard to see anything besides that dripping knife and Rudy's mocking smile.

Every little sound was magnified a thousand-fold. After the first couple of times, when Julie realized she was startling birds and rodents out of their homes, she bit her lip to avoid crying out and giving away her location. Then again, with the amount of racket she was creating maybe he'd think a bear was wandering the area. God, she hoped not. She couldn't handle any more predators at the moment, thank you very much.

Something about the angel seemed familiar, but she couldn't place him. And here she was, running full tilt down the side of a mountain with a madman on her trail wondering where she'd seen a spirit before, like that wasn't crazy—much.

The truck came into view and her heart sped up. Now that she was within reach of safety the danger seemed magnified. Her hands turned clammy. She couldn't hear for the buzzing in her ears, and her knees wobbled.

C'mon, Crenshaw, keep it together. Just a little further, you can do this. You have *to do this.*

Julie slowed and edged to the side of the trail, her eyes peeled for anything that moved. She had a good-sized stick she'd grabbed on the way down, but it wouldn't be much of a deterrent against a butcher knife.

Ron lay where he'd fallen, in a little clearing about ten feet from the passenger side of the truck. He wasn't moving.

She muffled a cry with her fist. They hadn't gotten along very well, but she hated the thought of him dying on the ground like that. Maybe she could get him to the truck? The distance stretched to football field proportions, but she had no choice. She wasn't leaving without him.

Her body hunched to create as small a target as possible, Julie duck-walked her way to Ron's side. She huddled against his back and searched the forest, her breath streaming in and out like a locomotive. When nothing stirred in the vicinity, she took a chance and concentrated her attention on Henderson. He lay on his side, his hands curled around his stomach as though to protect vital organs. The nice white dress shirt he'd worn this morning was now brick-red. He'd lost a lot of blood.

She placed two fingers against his throat and held her breath. There. Thready, but proof that he was alive. Now to get him to wake up so he could help her because there was no way she could lift him into the truck even if she could somehow drag him that far. All without being heard by a psychotic killer.

If only she could call Connor.

Her gaze went to the truck. Was it worth the chance? Only one way to find out.

"Hold on, Ron," she whispered. "Help is on the way."

God, she hoped she was right.

CHAPTER THIRTY-FIVE

Connor drove like an Indy champion, his guts twisted into a tight ball of foreboding. What if he was too late? No, he refused to believe that monster had gotten hold of Julie. It was mindboggling the son-of-a-bitch had been under their noses the entire time and they hadn't known it.

Rudy Franklin Ford.

When Matt said he'd gone back to the tattoo parlor on his own, Connor was pissed. Anything could have happened. The perp might even have shown up to finish the job. They were a team, dammit, he should have called it in. On the other hand, his quick thinking might have saved Julie's life.

They'd met up with Maddie in the empty Crenshaw home and Matt explained how Marko had been persuaded to describe his client if he wanted to remain open without the Health and Safety Board down his neck. As soon as Matt figured out who he was talking about, he'd raced to Julie's house, aware that she was friends with the Fords. His intention was to sit in surveillance on the hunch that Rudy would show up, then call for back-up.

Unfortunately, Rudy got the drop on him when he nodded off, still suffering the after-effects of his concussion. He'd held a gun and forced Matt into the trunk, then knocked him over the head. When Matt came to, he'd been trussed up like a fricken turkey.

Maddie had tsk-tsked, checking him out over Matt's arguments, while Connor searched for clues, his heart in his throat. Some files on the coffee table pointed to the story she'd been working on—The ABC Killer.

Dammit, what was she doing?

Then he saw the report she'd prepared with the Mayor of Sooke, and he knew. She took great satisfaction in her job, thoroughness was essential.

She'd gone to the last crime scene.

Frustration warred with pride. She was a stubborn, aggravating, thoroughly intoxicating woman. And he wanted her and the boys in his life. Needed her to trust him enough to give him a chance.

Why hadn't she let him know what she was doing?

He could have gone with her; made sure she was safe. He pressed down on the gas pedal and glanced at the grimly silent man in the passenger seat. "Don't beat yourself up, you did what you thought was best."

Matt shook his head and stared out the window.

Maddie leaned forward from her position in the back and squeezed Connor's shoulder. "It'll be okay. We'll find her."

He met her worried gaze in the rearview mirror and knew she was thinking the same as him—if the killer didn't get there first.

Finally, they arrived at the forestry road. The rain had dampened the dust, but it had also turned the road to snot, making it all but impossible to navigate. When they almost kissed a tree for the third time, Connor slammed the car in park and smacked the steering wheel. "I can't get any closer, we're going to have to hike the rest of the way."

Maddie opened her door. "How much further?"

Connor climbed out and waited for Matt to join them at the trunk. "Suit up. It's about five miles up the mountain, but we don't know what to expect so we better go in prepared for trouble."

They pulled on flak jackets, and Matt grabbed a Smith and Wesson while Connor switched his Sig for the Winchester.

When they were ready, Connor closed the lid, careful to keep the noise down and nodded to the trail winding through the trees. "We should split up; we'll cover more ground. I'll take the trail, you guys go by the road, but for God's sake, be careful. We don't know if Ford is here or not, or what he has for weaponry."

Matt held out his hand. "See you on the other side."

The rain had eased to a drizzle, but now it started to come down again as though someone above had turned the tap on full-blast. Big fat plops drenched their shoulders and faces and created an impenetrable mist, adding to the shit-factor by oh-a-thousand-or so craptastics. This day was just getting better and better.

Connor shook his friend's hand, then nodded to Maddie. "Keep him in line and watch your back."

She smiled, though her eyes remained serious. "Will do, sir. Be careful out there."

The danger was all too real. There was a possibility one of them could be hurt, maybe even seriously. They were trained for these kinds of scenarios, knew what to do, how to react, but, given Murphy's Law, Connor wasn't surprised she was worried.

A faint cry punctuated the fog. Connor's heart stopped.

Julie.

He shared a last grim glance with Matt and Maddie, then turned and trotted into the woods, praying like he'd never prayed before.

CHAPTER THIRTY-SIX

Julie's heart pounded against the wall of her chest, harder than the rain that had begun to fall in buckets, soaking her to the skin and making visibility next to nothing. She glanced at Ron again, grateful he was lying on his side. At least he wouldn't drown. Not that it would matter for much longer if she didn't get him some help.

She nudged him, hoping against hope he'd wake up, jump to his feet, and take over getting them out of here in his usual bossy, sarcastic way, but it was no go. He didn't even flinch. She was on her own.

C'mon, Jules, you can do this.

Mike. She closed her eyes and lifted her face to the rain, heedless of the icy pellets striking her skin. His spirit infused her body, pushing away the cold and the fear.

He was here. She could feel his presence, a warm blanket wrapping her in a cocoon of safety and love. He'd come to her on a couple of other occasions. Times when she wanted to give up, her will to live gone. He'd held her then too, and soothed the ache. Healed her pain by letting her know she wasn't alone. And it helped. She missed him and baby Ava more than she could say, but at least they weren't gone forever. His spirit lived on, and maybe one day, they'd all be together again.

Just not today. Her eyes opened and she scanned the clearing through the gathering fog. Her kids needed her for a few more years—and there was Connor.

Infused with a burst of hope, she left Ron's side and started her run across the distance to the looming outline of the pick-up. If she could just reach her phone…

A shape burst out of the gloom and slammed into her from the right, sending her flying into the scrub. She shrieked, getting a glimpse of Rudy. Rage turned the average-looking face into a mask filled with hatred. It was impossible to reconcile this monster with the man who brought toys for her kids and fixed her plumbing when it went wonky.

He lunged after her. She let out another screech and rolled away, the brush catching in her hair and scratching exposed skin. Her fingers scrambled for purchase over the mud and rocks, desperate to gain enough leeway that she could regain her footing.

He slipped and fell, his grunt audible even through the pounding pulse in her ears. She grabbed her chance and stumbled to her feet, swaying under shock from the attack. He was already up, heading her way, when she gathered enough wits to turn and run.

Corporal Tate stood a few yards away, feet spread, and a nasty looking gun pointed right at her.

Julie screamed.

Then immediately choked it off, because of course the gun was pointed her way, just not *at* her.

And sure enough, Corporal Tate raised the gun enough to show she meant business and warned Rudy to freeze. "You move one inch and I'll blow a hole in you the size of the Bermuda Triangle," she growled. "You okay, Mrs. Crenshaw?"

Julie nodded, relieved. The familiar touch of her husband's hand on her shoulder caused her to sag to her knees. A breath of cool air against her cheek and his whispered warning, "Stay down," came seconds before the deafening report of a gunshot. Screeching, she ducked, covering her head. When she looked up, she expected to see the Corporal's gun smoking. Instead, she saw a shocked look of pain on the woman's face as bright red color ballooned on her neck and she toppled backward without a sound.

Oh, my God. She's dead. He has a gun. He's going to kill me.

The panicked thoughts roared through her head like a freight train. She'd never seen anyone murdered before. It was worse than television. Way worse.

No, he's not.

Julie couldn't tell if the voice in her head was her or Mike, but it gave her the courage to fight. If she was going to die anyway, at least she could make it hard for him. She heard Rudy behind her and gasped. Expecting a bullet in the back at any moment, she scrambled to her feet, and almost made it away before he grasped her hair and yanked, dragging her backward against his body.

She shuddered.

"Hello, sweetheart." His voice in her ear so soon after Mike's was like a rape to her senses. The horror didn't set in until she saw the knife he held when his arm snaked around her chest.

She whimpered. "Please, Rudy, just let me go."

He rubbed his chin against her cheek, the bristles abrading her skin. "Now where's the fun in that?"

She caught movement from the corner of her eye, and it took every ounce of self-control she could muster, not to scream for help. It was only a matter of time before Rudy figured out an RCMP officer wouldn't be up here on her own. Somehow, Julie needed to keep him busy until whoever it was—she prayed for Connor, at the same time hoping he stayed away—could get into a position to help her.

"Does Sam know what you are?" God she hoped not.

His arm tightened. "Leave Sam out of this. Your kind don't deserve to be in the same room with her." The butt of the knife dug into her belly, robbing her of air.

He gave a push with his groin and she gagged.

He laughed.

"What's the matter? Think I'm not good enough for you?" The push became a shove, knocking her off her balance, to land on the ground at his feet. "You're all the same," he growled. "Unless we're physically perfect, you don't give us a second goddamn glance."

His gait was uneven as he moved to stand over her, and she gaped. Why hadn't she ever seen this before? He'd hidden it well, but now the pieces were falling into place.

"What happened, Rudy? How did you lose your foot?" Any sympathy she might have felt was superseded by the fact that he had become a killer due to his defect.

He stared down at her, but she could see his thoughts were on some horrid accident from the past.

His brows scrunched as though in pain, and his lips peeled back in a snarl. "My dear mother thought it was fitting punishment when I disobeyed a direct command."

Julie gasped, horrified.

Rudy refocused, and just for a moment it was her old friend standing before her again. She reached out in empathy. He recoiled. The light in his eyes died, and the monster returned.

He smiled, the knife glittering dully at his side. "Don't worry, honey. I learned from my lesson. Women like you, ones who think they're too good for the rest of us, they need taught, just like I was."

"Stop. Drop your weapon." Connor's voice rang out from the shadows. "This is the police. You are under arrest."

Rudy froze.

Julie waited, her heart in her throat. He stared at her for a long moment, then a look of peace turned his face almost serene. *Thank God.* He was going to turn himself in.

The thought no more than crossed her mind when he turned, raised the knife over his head, and screamed while rushing in Connor's direction.

"Connor," Julie cried, even as the blast from a rifle split the air.

Rudy stumbled, took a few uneven steps, and collapsed.

Connor rose from his position behind a giant cedar, and met her gaze across the distance.

It was over.

CHAPTER THIRTY-SEVEN

Connor was a trained professional with more than twelve years on the force, but all of that flew out the window the moment he cleared a knoll and came upon a scene straight out of his worst nightmares.

Julie lay on the ground, her cameraman, Rudy, standing with a bloody knife over her prone body. His skin went icy with a fear unlike any he'd ever known. It took every ounce of control he could grasp not to go racing out there like a madman. But that would only endanger the woman he loved more than life itself. He needed to keep calm. Think.

He took some deep, cleansing breaths, lowered himself behind a blind, and set up the rifle over a fallen log. He centered the sight on Julie's frightened face and his heart pinched. He'd shifted the scope until he had a clear shot and did his job. It was between him and God whether he shot Ford out of necessity or desire.

When it was over, the suspect lay dead. Julie ran to his side, sobs shaking her slender form. He wrapped his arms around her and just held on, grateful to whoever was listening that she was alive. He made a silent promise to devote his life to making her and the boys happy. He never wanted to go through something like this again.

"Shh, honey, don't cry." He ran a tender hand under her wet hair and rubbed her back. "I've got you, you're safe now. You're safe."

Then he remembered the blood on the knife and his heart stopped. He pushed her away so he could check her over. "Are you hurt?" he demanded, and cursed when she flinched at his harsh tone. He lowered his voice and asked again, gently this time. "Julie, honey, you need to tell me where you're hurt so I can help you."

She stared at him, her eyes blank with shock. "What?" She looked down at her mud-caked clothes and dirty, scratched toes in a silly pair of light-weight sandals. A full-body shudder rattled her teeth. Her beautiful green-gold eyes were liquid with despair. "It was Rudy. He ki... killed Ron and Officer Tate."

Her misery broke his heart. He kissed her brow. "I'm so sorry, honey. I know he was your friend." The betrayal and loss would haunt her for a long time, but he planned on being there when she needed him. If she would let him.

"I have to go check on the others, are you sure you're all right?" He waited until she nodded, then helped her over to a four-by-four sitting nearby. When he opened the passenger door he saw her purse on the floor and sighed. No wonder she hadn't answered his calls.

"Sit here, where it's dry. I won't be long, okay?" He made sure she was settled, then closed the door and made his way over to Ford. His shot had been true. He'd known by the man's jagged gait that he was dying, but needed to be sure. He did a quick visual, careful not to touch anything, and was about to move on when he noticed the awkward angle of the man's left ankle. A closer inspection proved him to be an amputee. Connor figured the story behind the loss of his foot was probably at the root of his psychological break. In his experience, it was generally a childhood drama that twisted something in the minds of psychopaths and sent them down the road of murder and mayhem.

Satisfied this one was done with his spree, Connor moved on and searched for Maddie. He found her a short distance away, flat on her back, eyes gazing sightlessly at the crying skies.

Damn.

He leaned over and brushed her lids closed. She'd been in his department for just over two years, young, smart, and a damn fine officer. He was going to miss her.

Reluctantly, he turned away and began the final search for the reporter Julie had traveled with. Matt broke cover when he was halfway through the first quadrant.

"Where the hell have you been?" Connor growled.

Matt reared back. "What's your problem, man? Maddie and I split up to cover more area. I heard shots and came as quick as I could." He glanced around. "You get him?"

Connor lifted his chin toward the fallen man. "Yeah."

Matt relaxed and grinned. "Way to go. Another scumbag bites the dust. Where's your girlfriend? Maddie take her home?"

Oh shit.

Connor slowly shook his head. "She didn't make it, Matt. Maddie's gone."

Matt's smile flat-lined. "What do you mean, gone?" He stared at Connor. "You're one sick fuck, you know that right? That's not funny, man. Where is she?"

Connor nodded to where he'd left Maddie. He sighed, his chest heavy as his friend stumbled across the distance and fell to his knees by her side. His shoulders shook as he reached out to touch her, his head bowed.

Connor turned away to give him some privacy. If not for the grace of God that could be him kneeling in the mud with his love fading away forever.

He shuddered.

A low moan off to his left jerked his attention to a dark mound all but hidden in a clump of ferns. Henderson.

He hurried over, relieved Ron was still alive.

"Hang on, help is on the way," Connor said, though he didn't think the man heard him. The entire right side of his shirt was soaked in blood, his skin was pasty, the pulse weak and thready. He needed immediate attention.

"Matt," he called. "Hurry, I need help." While he had basic medical training, Matt was much more proficient and would be better suited to keeping Henderson alive until emergency services could arrive.

Matt glared over his shoulder, but got to his feet and made his way over, swiping his eyes with the sleeve of his jacket. "What do you have?"

Connor kept his professional mask on, aware his friend wouldn't appreciate his sympathy at the moment. "White male. Thirty to thirty-five years of age. Stab victim. Looks to be through the right side. I can't tell without moving him if it went through or not."

Matt nodded and bent for a better look. "Yeah, it's bad. I can do compression, but he needs help like yesterday."

Connor pulled out his satellite phone and called it in. "Do what you can. I'm going to check on Julie. You good here?"

Matt kept working, his head down. "Yeah, see to your lady." He glanced up. "Give her a hug for me, will ya?"

Connor swallowed hard. "Sure, buddy. I'll do that." This job sucked sometimes. There was no telling when your ticket might get pulled. A simple traffic stop turned to road rage, or a murderous killer with nothing to lose. It was all a crapshoot.

Maybe it was time he moved on. He wanted to spend his life with Julie, watch the kids grow up, maybe even have one or two of his own. Funny, he never saw himself as anything other than a cop, wasn't even sure he could be happy at another occupation. But then she came into view, her gorgeous eyes filled with relief—and dare he hope, love?—and he knew it didn't really matter what he did for work, as long as he had her to come home to at night, his life would be full.

***

Mike watched the scene being played out between his wife and the cop with a bittersweet mix of emotions churning in his gut. He was happy she'd found someone new, a guy who was willing to put her and the boys first in his life. Yes, he'd read the man's mind, who could blame him? At the same time, he couldn't help but wonder what his place in their lives would become. Would they forget him?

"You know that's not going to happen," Lucas said, landing next to him. "Your family will *always* be your family. Love is magical that way. It stretches until it can encompass everyone in its embrace." He clasped Mike's shoulder and nodded toward the cop. "He'll take good care of them for you."

Yeah, he would.

Lucas moved off to dispatch the spirit of the killer to the lower levels under Transition House. He had a long way to go before the Lord would grant him passage to a higher plane.

Mike waited for the young corporal's soul to leave her body. Sometimes, like in Lucas' case, the spirit became confused with the change. It was his job to smooth the way, make their shift easier. Help them to understand their new roles. He thought back to the connection he'd made with Madison Tate. Maybe, on some level she'd known her days were limited and it had allowed her to see him when others could not.

He liked her. She had spunk. It would be interesting showing her his world. And maybe, not so lonely.

He took one more look at Julie, then followed Maddie's spirit up to Heaven.

Reviews are the lifeblood of any successful author. Without you, we can't be heard.

If you enjoy the story, please consider sharing on your favorite social media sites, as well as GoodReads and from wherever you've bought the book.

Thank you,

Jacquie Biggar

Jacqbiggar.com

About the Author

JACQUIE BIGGAR is a USA Today bestselling author of Romantic Suspense who loves to write about tough, alpha males who know what they want, that is until they're gob-smacked by heroines who are strong, contemporary women willing to show them what they really need is love. She is the author of the popular Wounded Hearts series and has just started a new series in paranormal suspense, Mended Souls.

She has been blessed with a long, happy marriage and enjoys writing romance novels that end with happily-ever-afters.

Jacquie lives in paradise along the west coast of Canada with her family and loves reading, writing, and flower gardening. She swears she can't function without coffee, preferably at the beach with her sweetheart. :)

Free reads, excerpts, author news, and contests can be found on her web site:

http://jacqbiggar.com

You can follow her on at http://Facebook.com/jacqbiggar , http://Twitter.com/jacqbiggar

Or email her via her web site. Jacquie lives on Vancouver Island with her husband and loves to hear from readers all over the world!

You can also join her street team on Facebook: Biggar's Book Buddies

And sign up for her newsletter-
http://eepurl.com/2MFvX